ARCHETYPES OF THE COLLECTIVE UNCONSCIOUS
VOLUME 4
Reflecting American Culture Through Literature and Art

LOVER

EMBRACING OUR PASSIONATE HEARTS

Introduction by Robert A. Johnson

JEREMY P. TARCHER/PUTNAM
A MEMBER OF PENGUIN PUTNAM INC.
NEW YORK

A BOOK LABORATORY BOOK

Most Tarcher/Putnam books are available at special quantity discounts for bulk purchase for sales promotions, premiums, fund-raising, and educational needs. Special books or book excerpts also can be created to fit specific needs. For details, write Putnam Special Markets, 375 Hudson Street, New York, NY 10014.

Jeremy P. Tarcher/Putnam
A member of
Penguin Putnam Inc.
375 Hudson Street
New York, NY 10014
www.penguinputnam.com
Introduction © Robert A. Johnson
Searching for Love Through Stories and Art © Mark Robert Waldman
Designed by Kristen Garneau, Garneau Design, Sausalito, CA

Library of Congress Cataloging-in-Publications Data

Lover: embracing the passionate heart / introduction by Robert A. Johnson.
        p. cm.—(Archetypes of the collective unconscious ; v. 4)
      "A Book Laboratory book"—T.p. verso
    ISBN 1-58542-190-1
      1. Love stories, American. I. Series.
   PS648.L6L74 2002   2002028704
810.8′03543—dc21

Printed in Singapore
10 9 8 7 6 5 4 3 2 1

TABLE OF CONTENTS

ABOUT THIS SERIES

O UR WORLD IS FILLED WITH ARCHETYPAL IMAGERY, POWERFUL SYMBOLS THAT REFLECT THE DEEPEST LAYERS OF OUR personality—our strengths, weaknesses, and unacknowledged gifts that lay hidden within our souls. Primarily unconscious, these inner forces shape our behaviors, attitudes, and beliefs. By exploring these secret desires—in ourselves, through literature and art—we can gain mastery over them, bringing greater consciousness into our lives.

Archetypal themes are universal, for they can be found in every culture throughout history. But each society reflects them in distinctive ways. The American lover, for example, is far more romantic, erotic, and idealized than the images portrayed in Asia. By contrast, the shadow, which is aptly acknowledged in the European psyche, is relatively ignored by Americans. Unlike other cultures, we do not like to peer directly at the darkness that lies within. Instead we project our shadows onto fiction, the movies, or the criminal elements in the world. Even the shadow artists in America are often met with hostility or disdain, especially when the subject offends our moral and religious values. The shadow artist is readily condemned, an unpatriotic pariah that spoils our fantasies and dreams.

The American seeker is also unique amongst the cultures of the world: in our separation of church from state, religion becomes a quest for personal spirituality, one that liberally borrows from other traditions and groups. Our economic and scientific advancements have also transformed the healer archetype from a country shaman into a medical sage.

Artists, poets, and writers help to bring these archetypal forms to life by embracing them in their work. Stephen King, for example, is a master of the shadow, as was Sexton, Poe, and Melville. The spiritual quest of the seeker is vividly captured in the poetry of Whitman and Frost, in the prose of Alice Walker, and in the speeches of Martin Luther King. Even the face of Andrew Weil, alternative medicine's champion, has become a core archetypal symbol of the American healer: wise, warm, and passionately devoted to the integration of body, mind, and soul. And who would not be moved by O. Henry's *The Gift of the Magi* in which two lovers sacrifice their most valued possessions to soothe each other's hearts?

Art in particular makes a strong impression upon our soul, and in choosing the illustrations to accompany these stories, we have selected unique images that span the breadth and depth of contemporary American painting and photography. From the sun-dappled colors of the impressionists, to the austere contrasts of black and white photography, and from the immediacy of the advertising medium to the obliqueness of the symbolic form, these images hint at the acuity of our inner landscapes and dreams. Mysterious, moody, and serene, they work upon our psyches inviting us to rest the eye upon the symbolic eloquence of life. The volumes in this series highlight the artistry of America's collective spirit.

May these stories and images guide you inwards as you witness that wondrous place where a greater consciousness resides.

The wonder of the collective unconscious is that it is all there, all the legend and history of the human race, with its unexorcised demons and its gentle saints, its mysteries and its wisdom, all with each one of us—a microcosm with the macrocosm. The exploration of this world is more challenging than the exploration of the solar system; and the journey to inner space is not necessarily an easy or a safe trip.

—June Singer

The archetype represents a profound riddle surpassing our rational comprehension [expressing] itself first and foremost in metaphors. There is some part of its meaning that always remains unknown and defies formulation.

—Jacobi Jolande

Our personal psychology is just a thin skin, a ripple on the ocean of collective psychology [and] the archetypes are the great decisive forces, they bring about the real events, and not our personal reasoning and practical intellect . . . . The archetypal images decide the fate of man.

—Carl G. Jung

Series Editor: Mark Robert Waldman
Series conceived by Jeremy P. Tarcher
Series created by Philip Dunn, Manuela Dunn Mascetti and Book Laboratory
Picture research by Julie Foakes
Design by Kristen Garneau

Other Titles in the Series:
Shadow: Touching the Darkness Within, Volume 1, with an Introduction by Robert Bly
Healer: Transforming Our Inner and Outer Wounds, Volume 2, with an Introduction by Andrew Weil
Seeker: Traveling the Path to Enlightenment, Volume 3, with an Introduction by Jean Houston

R O M A N C E   A N D   T H E
A R C H E T Y P E   O F   L O V E

by Robert A. Johnson

THE LOVER IS ONE OF THE MOST POTENT ARCHETYPAL FORCES IN THE WESTERN PSYCHE, AND IN AMERICA, ROMANTIC love may well be the single greatest energy system that governs our lives, competing with religion as the arena in which we seek meaning, wholeness, and ecstasy. Nearly every level of the entertainment world—our movies, novels, magazines and media advertising—taps into this hunger, the *passio perpetua* of the modern age. At its best, romantic love leads us past the literalism and materialism of the Western mind and brings us face to face with the symbolic life, opening our eyes to the meaning of human love. At its worst, it distorts and wastes our lives.

In our culture, our ideals have been set so high that we have come to believe that romantic love is the only form of "love" on which marriage and intimacy can be based. Other cultures, like those of India and Japan, foster deep love and devotion for their partners, but they do not impose the kinds of impossible demands and expectations as Americans have done, believing, as we so often do when we "fall in love," that we have found the ultimate meaning of life. We feel completed—as if we have found the missing parts of ourselves—and we suddenly feel alive and whole. But when the fantasy wears off, we become anxious, angry, or depressed. We blame our partners for the loss of ecstatic love, or seek romance with someone new.

Underneath, we do not recognize the deep sense of loneliness and alienation that emerges from this idealistic pursuit, one which limits our ability to form genuinely loving and committed relationships. Romance insinuates that we have the right to expect that our desires can and should be satisfied. But by its very nature, romance must deteriorate into egotism, for it speaks more about our own fantasies, projections, and expectations than it does of the other person.

This is the great wound of our psyche, and if we are to heal ourselves, we must undertake the difficult task of understanding it. This path towards consciousness can bring new awareness about ourselves and our relationships with others.

Romantic love has overwhelmed our collective psyche, permanently altering our view of the world. As a society, we have not yet learned to handle the tremendous power of romantic love, yet if we are to find true and lasting love, we must look honestly at these ideals we have projected onto others. Such a journey into the archetypal realms of love will force us to look not only at the beauty and potential in romantic love but also at the illusions we hold inside. In this process of self-discovery, we may have to make profound changes in our attitudes and beliefs in order to allow a deeper human love to take hold.

Because love is an archetype, it has its own personality and traits. Like a god, love behaves like a separate being in the psyche, acting from within and enabling us to look beyond ourselves at our fellow human beings—people who can be valued and cherished, rather than used. Love is not so much something I do as something that I am. It is a state of being through which I am connected with another living being, and the love that flows through me is independent of my intentions or desire.

Love is greater, deeper and more profound than anything I may wish it to be, for its existence does not depend upon me or the beliefs that I may try to impose upon it. Human love transcends the illusions of romantic love, but it has become so obscured by our passions that we hardly know what to look for when we seek genuine intimacy with others. But if we look closely, we may begin to feel the spontaneous flow of warmth that surges towards another person in the small unnoticed acts of life: the ways in which we value the other as a total, individual self and our acceptance of their imperfections and faults. When we truly love another, we love their shadow side as well.

Human love causes us to see the intrinsic value in each other, and it awakens the ego to a power that is greater than ourselves. This type of love

To be capable of real love means becoming mature, with realistic expectations of the other person. It means accepting responsibility for our own happiness or unhappiness, and neither expecting the other person to make us happy nor blaming that person for our moods and frustrations.

—John A. Sanford, *Invisible Partners*

empowers us to honor each other, to serve each other rather than use. As Saint Paul wrote, " Love does not envy; love does not vaunt itself, is not puffed up . . . . Love bears all things, believes all things, hopes all things, endures all things."

A wise friend once referred to this kind of love as "stirring the oatmeal"—a humble act that brings love down to earth, and which embraces a willingness to share the simple and ordinary tasks of life. To "stir the oatmeal" means to find the relatedness in managing the budget, parenting one's children, and handling the day-to-day stresses of work rather than seeking the extraordinary intensity of romance. Like the rice hulling of the Zen monks, the spinning wheel of Gandhi, the tent making of Saint Paul, it represents the discovery of the sacred in the midst of the humble and ordinary.

Real relatedness is experienced in the small tasks we do together, in the daily companionship and in the quiet conversations at the end of the day, in the gentle words of encouragement we offer in difficult times.

The stories in this book speak deeply about modern love, of our romantic ideals and the pain we suffer when our desires are not met, but they also hint at our potential to transcend these illusions and touch upon the deeper layers of love. In these tales you will see how we look for something more than the man or woman in front of us: we project onto our love a divine and perfect image, a passion that goes beyond physical attraction, beyond love, to a sense of worship. We seek the "spiritual" intensity, the ecstasy and the despair, the joyous meetings and the tearful partings—the "specialness" that comes with romance. But we cannot linger forever in the romantic ideal; eventually we must push forward to overcome the dogmas of our culture. Nor can we solve our problems by imitating attitudes from abroad. We have to deal with our own Western unconscious and our own Western wounds, finding the healing balm within our own Western soul. What we will find is that the essence of happiness is not so much to be loved, as to love.

As a society, [Americans] face a collective loneliness, an empty feeling that comes . . . from the loss of meaningful interaction, the failure to be part of something real.

—Laura Pappano

Right: Andrew Lane, *Untitled.*

S E A R C H I N G   F O R   L O V E   T H R O U G H
S T O R I E S   A N D   A R T

by Mark Robert Waldman, Series Editor

Why is it that we delight most of all in some tale of impossible love? Because we long for the branding; because we long to grow aware of what is on fire inside us.

—Denis de Rougemont, *Love in the Western World*

We dream an impossible dream of embracing the ideal lover in our arms. And for most Americans, it is a dream from which we never awake, for no archetypal force feels more powerful, more pervasive—more mysterious—than love.

Since the dawn of history, the lover has appeared in all great literature and art, yet it is an image that never fully rises into consciousness. Thus the lover acts upon us in seemingly irrational ways, driving us into beds of passion and courts of bitter divorce. "Love is the great intangible," Diane Ackerman writes. " Frantic and serene, vigilant and calm, wrung-out and fortified, explosive and sedate—love commands a vast army of moods."

The lover has taken many forms throughout history: she has been both virgin and seductress, goddess and whore; he has been a rapist and a knight, a passionate troubadour who never consummates his lust. Images of the lover have adorned great temples in the East, but in the West, the lover's potency has been challenged by the church, for earthly pleasures were seen as detractors from the higher pursuit of the soul. This is the boiling pot into which Americans are thrown, torn between an antiquated Puritan ethic and a rapacious thirst for romance, living in a culture where sex and love are inextricably tied.

Through our literature and art, through movies and commercial advertising, we are setting the tone for the rest of the world. In America, we have freed the archetypal lover from historical restraints: she is more sensual than women who are raised in other cultures, more romantic, idealistic, and seductive; he is more dependent and attached, less macho, more soft. Even in marriage, we demand more from our partners than other cultures expect. We ask for companionship *and* friendship, empathy *and* personal space, and we want to be deeply understood. To a fault, we believe that happiness can be found solely through an intimate bond, for we are the only country in the world that equates marriage with romantic love.

Are our ideals too high? The question is open to debate: some point an accusatory finger at the national divorce rate, which, for decades, has hovered around fifty percent. Others suggest that we simply haven't learned how to listen, or to effectively communicate our needs. Our bookstores brim with self-help books promoting fabulous romance, profound intimacy and permanent love, but our songs are filled with heartbreak. To others outside of our culture, we appear to vacillate between extreme idealism and emotional pain, longing for rich relationships but wary of commitments. Laura Pappano, author of *The Connection Gap: Why Americans Feel So Alone,* writes:

> *We are a bundle of contradictions, eager to feel rooted but finding ourselves willingly pulled along with the tide. As a society we face a collective loneliness, an empty feeling that comes not from lack of all human interaction, but from the loss of meaningful interaction, the failure to be a part of something real, or to have faith in institutions that might bring us together.*

Other scholars believe that our passionate pursuits reflect the essence of archetypal love. "In the aspirations of romantic love," says Jungian analyst Robert A. Johnson, "there is a deep psychological truth that reverberates in our souls, that awakens us to what we are at our best, what we are when we are whole." Loyalty and commitment are also needed, Johnson adds: "It is out of this profound human need for stable, loyal, and enduring relationships that the morality of commitment grows."

The archetype of the American lover has its darkness as well: in child pornography, in date rapes and emotional abuse, in the casual affairs of the heart that threaten the security of our homes. There are the "fatal attractions" as well: women and men who continue to violate the boundaries of intimacy and trust. Teenage

America is particularly vulnerable to the lover's shadow through relentless marketing of clothing and cosmetics which link sensuality with love. Sadly, our corporate structure seems to feed upon our obsessions with beauty and age, and the images they produce push us towards an endless anxiety, fostering eating disorders, addictions, depression, even death. Teen magazines continue to promote illusions that feminists have fought for decades to dissolve: fantasies of the ideal orgasm, the ideal marriage, the ideal woman and man. Such promises fail to prepare our youth for the difficult issues relationships impose. Romance and sensuality may open the doors to love, but the skills that are needed to maintain intimacy, resolve conflicts and insure domestic autonomy require dedicated perseverance—a perspective that few young lovers have. The fairy tale, *Stubborn Husband, Stubborn Wife,* which appears in this volume, humorously reflects a dilemma that so many couples face.

Despite the potential for disillusionment and pain, we remain optimistic in our search for romance and love. We marry, divorce, and remarry, gaining from our prior mistakes. These archetypal forces of love drive us to greater depths and heights.

This anthology opens with O. Henry's classic tale, *The Gift of the Magi,* an ageless allegory which captures the love that is buried in the American soul, of two people who sacrifice the objects they cherish in order to soothe the other's pain. In Debra Boxer's *Innocence in Extremis,* we witness a young woman's dream for the ideal sexual embrace. And in the stories by Twain, Gunn Allen, Miller, and Gildner, we explore the beginning stages of dating and romance, culminating with William Sansom's portrayal of the inevitable first kiss. These stories hold out the promise of sex, but the prevailing issues revolve around intimacy, longing and trust.

In American literature, the shadow sides of love are often punctuated with humor. This darkness is brilliantly executed in Thurber's and

Romantic love requires courage— the courage to stay vulnerable, to stay open to our feelings for our partner, even when we are temporarily in conflict, even we are frustrated, hurt, angry—the courage to remain connected with our love, rather than shut down emotionally, even when it is terribly difficult to do so.

—Nathaniel Branden

Roger's tales, in which two husbands ponder the future of their marital fates. One chooses murder, the other goes home with someone else's mate. Darker themes are equally employed by Kilpatrick and Poe. Whitman's poem, *To a Common Prostitute*, and the traditional folk ballad, *Frankie and Johnnie*, also bewitch us with the darker sides of love, which is taken by Oates into the land of social taboo: the seduction of a young boy by his teacher.

Memories of loves regretted and lost can be found in Davis's reminiscence of divorce in *The Sock* and in Uyematsu's poem, *To Women Who Sleep Alone*. Love, too, is savored in Fulghum's obsession with a misplaced cigar, then taken to absurdity in Frazier's Freudian whim, *Dating Your Mom*. From the unspoiled dreams of our adolescent past, to the yearning for love yet found, these stories and poems help to illuminate the fires that linger in our hearts.

Passionate lovers experience [a] roller coaster of feelings euphoria, happiness, calm tranquility, vulnerability, anxiety, panic, despair . . . . fueled by a sprinkling of hope and a large dollop of loneliness, mourning, jealousy, and terror.

—Elaine Hatfield

THE GIFT OF THE MAGI

O. Henry

ONE DOLLAR AND EIGHTY-SEVEN CENTS. THAT WAS ALL. AND SIXTY CENTS OF it was in pennies. Pennies saved one and two at a time by bulldozing the grocer and the vegetable man and the butcher until one's cheeks burned with the silent imputation of parsimony that such close dealing implied. Three times Della counted it. One dollar and eighty-seven cents. And the next day would be Christmas.

There was clearly nothing to do but flop down on the shabby little couch and howl. So Della did it. Which instigates the moral reflection that life is made up of sobs, sniffles, and smiles, with sniffles predominating.

While the mistress of the home is gradually subsiding from the first stage to the second, take a look at the home. A furnished flat at $8 per week. It did not exactly beggar description, but it certainly had that word on the lookout for the mendicancy squad.

Right: Elizabeth Taylor and Richard Burton at a press conference in Los Angeles, 1963. During the course of their stormy relationship, he sometimes gave her gifts so extravagant they made the news.

In the vestibule below was a letterbox into which no letter would go, and an electric button from which no mortal finger could coax a ring. Also appertaining thereunto was a card bearing the name "Mr. James Dillingham Young."

The "Dillingham" had been flung to the breeze during a former period of prosperity when its possessor was being paid $30 per week. Now, when the income was shrunk to $20, the letters of "Dillingham" looked blurred, as though they were thinking seriously of contracting to a modest and unassuming D. But whenever Mr. James Dillingham Young came home and reached his flat above he was called "Jim" and greatly hugged by Mrs. James Dillingham Young, already introduced to you as Della. Which is all very good.

Della finished her cry and attended to her cheeks with the powder rag. She stood by the window and looked out dully at a grey cat walking a grey fence in a grey backyard. Tomorrow would be Christmas Day, and she had only $1.87 with which to buy Jim a present. She had been saving every penny she could for months, with this result. Twenty dollars a week doesn't go far. Expenses had been greater than she had calculated. They always are. Only $1.87 to buy a present for Jim. Her Jim. Many a happy hour she had spent planning for something nice for him. Something fine and rare and sterling—something just a little bit near to being worthy of the honor of being owned by Jim.

There was a pier-glass between the windows of the room. Perhaps you have seen a pier-glass in an $8 flat. A very thin and very agile person may, by observing his reflection in a rapid sequence of longitudinal strips, obtain a fairly accurate conception of his looks. Della, being slender, had mastered the art.

Suddenly she whirled from the window and stood before the glass. Her eyes were shining brilliantly, but her face had lost its color within twenty seconds. Rapidly she pulled down her hair and let it fall to its full length.

Now, there were two possessions of the James Dillingham Youngs in which they both took a mighty pride. One was Jim's gold watch that had been his father's and grandfather's. The other was Della's hair. Had the Queen of Sheba lived in the flat across the airshaft, Della would have let her hair hang out the window some day to dry just to depreciate Her Majesty's jewels and gifts. Had King Solomon been the janitor, with all his treasures piled up in the basement, Jim would have pulled out his watch every time he passed, just to see him pluck at his beard from envy.

So now Della's beautiful hair fell about her, rippling and shining like a cascade of brown waters. It reached below her knee and made itself almost a garment for her. And then she did it up again nervously and quickly. Once she faltered for a minute and stood still while a tear or two splashed on the worn red carpet.

On went her old brown jacket; on went her old brown hat. With a whirl of skirts and with the brilliant sparkle still in her eyes, she fluttered out the door and down the stairs to the street.

Where she stopped the sign read: "Mme. Sofronie. Hair Goods of All Kinds." One flight up Della ran, and collected herself, panting. Madame, large, too white, chilly, hardly looked the "Sofronie."

"Will you buy my hair?" asked Della.

"I buy hair," said Madame. "Take yer hat off and let's have a sight at the looks of it."

Down rippled the brown cascade.

"Twenty dollars," said Madame, lifting the mass with a practiced hand.

"Give it to me quick," said Della.

Oh, and the next two hours tripped by on rosy wings. Forget the hashed metaphor. She was ransacking the stores for Jim's present.

She found it at last. It surely had been made for Jim and no one else. There was no other like it in any of the stores, and she had turned all of them inside out. It was a platinum fob chain simple and chaste in design, properly proclaiming its value by substance alone and not by meretricious ornamentation—as all good things should do. It was even worthy of The Watch. As soon as she saw it she knew that it must be Jim's. It was like him. Quietness and value—the description applied to both. Twenty-one dollars they took from her for it, and she hurried home with the 87 cents. With that chain on his watch Jim might be properly anxious about the time in any company. Grand as the watch was, he sometimes looked at it on the sly on account of the old leather strap that he used in place of a chain.

When Della reached home her intoxication gave way a little to prudence and reason. She got out her curling irons and lighted the gas and went to work repairing the ravages made by generosity added to love. Which is always a tremendous task, dear friends—a mammoth task.

Within forty minutes her head was covered with tiny, close-lying curls that made her look wonderfully like a truant school boy. She looked at her reflection in the mirror long, carefully, and critically.

"If Jim doesn't kill me," she said to herself, "before he takes a second look at me, he'll say I look like a Coney Island chorus girl. But what could I do—oh! what could I do with a dollar and eighty-seven cents?"

At 7 o'clock the coffee was made and the frying-pan was on, the back of the stove hot and ready to cook the chops.

Jim was never late. Della doubled the fob chain in her hand and sat on the corner of the table near the door that he always entered. Then she heard his step on the stair away down on the first flight, and she turned white for just a moment. She had a habit of saying little silent prayers about the simplest everyday things, and now she whispered: "Please God, make him think I am still pretty."

The door opened and Jim stepped in and closed it. He looked thin and very serious. Poor fellow, he was only twenty-two—and to be burdened with a family! He needed a new overcoat and he was without gloves.

Jim stopped inside the door, as immovable as a setter at the scent of quail. His eyes were fixed upon Della, and there was an expression in them that she could not read, and it terrified her. It was not anger, nor surprise, nor disapproval, nor horror, nor any of the sentiments that she had been prepared for. He simply stared at her fixedly with that peculiar expression on his face.

Della wriggled off the table and went for him.

"Jim, darling," she cried, "don't look at me that way. I had my hair cut off and sold it because I couldn't have lived through Christmas without giving you a present. It'll grow out again—you won't mind, will you? I just had to do it. My hair grows awfully fast. Say 'Merry Christmas!' Jim, and let's be happy. You don't know what a nice—what a beautiful, nice gift I've got for you."

"You've cut off your hair?" asked Jim, laboriously, as if he had not arrived at that patent fact yet even after the hardest mental labor.

"Cut it off and sold it," said Della. "Don't you like me just as well, anyhow? I'm me without my hair, ain't I?"

Jim looked about the room curiously.

"You say your hair is gone?' he said, with an air almost of idiocy.

"You needn't look for it," said Della. "It's sold, I tell you—sold and gone, too. It's Christmas Eve, boy. Be good to me, for it went for you. Maybe the hairs of my head were numbered," she went on with a sudden serious sweetness, "but nobody could ever count my love for you. Shall I put the chops on, Jim?"

Out of his trance Jim seemed quickly to wake. He enfolded his Della. For ten seconds let us regard with discreet scrutiny some inconsequential object in the other direction. Eight dollars a week or a million a year—what is the difference? A mathematician or a wit would give you the wrong answer. The magi brought valuable gifts, but that was not among them. This dark assertion will be illuminated later on.

Jim drew a package from his overcoat pocket and threw it upon the table.

"Don't make any mistake, Dell," he said, "about me. I don't think there's anything in the way of a haircut or a shave or a shampoo that could make me like my girl any less. But if you'll unwrap that package you may see why you had me going a while at first."

White fingers and nimble tore at the string and paper. And then an ecstatic scream of joy; and then, alas! a quick feminine change to hysterical tears and wails, necessitating the immediate employment of all the comforting powers of the lord of the flat.

For there lay The Combs—the set of combs, side and back, that Della had worshiped for so long in a Broadway window. Beautiful combs, pure tortoise shell, with jeweled rims—just the shade to wear in the beautiful vanished hair. They were expensive combs, she knew, and her heart had simply craved and yearned over them without the least hope of possession. And now, they were hers, but the tresses that should have adorned the coveted adornments were gone.

But she hugged them to her bosom, and at length she was able to look up with dim eyes and a smile and say: "My hair grows so fast, Jim!"

And then Della leaped up like a little singed cat and cried, "Oh, oh!"

Jim had not yet seen his beautiful present. She held it out to him eagerly upon her open palm. The dull precious metal seemed to flash with a reflection of her bright and ardent spirit.

"Isn't it a dandy, Jim? I hunted all over town to find it. You'll have to look at the time a hundred times a day now. Give me your watch. I want to see how it looks on it."

Instead of obeying, Jim tumbled down on the couch and put his hands under the back of his head and smiled.

"Dell," said he, "let's put our Christmas presents away and keep 'em a while. They're too nice to use just at present. I sold the watch to get the money to buy your combs. And now suppose you put the chops on."

The magi, as you know, were wise men—wonderfully wise men—who brought gifts to the Babe in the manger. They invented the art of giving Christmas presents. Being wise, their gifts were no doubt wise ones, possibly bearing the privilege of exchange in case of duplication. And here I have lamely related to you the uneventful chronicle of two foolish children in a flat who most unwisely sacrificed for each other the greatest treasures of their house. But in a last word to the wise of these days let it be said that of all who give gifts these two were the wisest. Of all who give and receive gifts, such as they are wisest. Everywhere they are wisest. They are the magi.

INNOCENCE IN EXTREMIS

Debra Boxer

I AM 28 YEARS OLD AND I AM A VIRGIN. PEOPLE ASSUME A SERIES OF DECISIONS LED TO THIS. THEY GUESS THAT I'M A CLOSET lesbian, or too picky, or clinging to a religious ideal. "You don't look, talk, or act like a virgin," they say. For lack of a better explanation, I am pigeonholed as a prude or an unfortunate. If it's so hard to believe, I want to say, then imagine how hard it is for me to live with.

I feel freakish and alien, an anomaly that belongs in a zoo. I walk around feeling like an impostor, not a woman at all. I bleed like other women, yet I feel nothing like them, because I am missing this formative experience.

I won't deny that I have become attached to my innocence. If it defines me, who am I without it? Where will my drive come from and what will protect me from becoming as jaded as everyone else? I try to tell myself that innocence is more a state of mind than body. That giving myself to a man doesn't mean losing myself to a cynical world. That my innocence doesn't hang by a scrap of skin between my legs.

In college, girls I knew lost it out of impatience. At 21, virginity became unhealthy, embarrassing—a female humiliation they could no longer be burdened by. Some didn't tell the boy. If there was blood, they said it was their period. I cannot imagine. Some of those same boys thought it was appalling, years ago, that I was still a virgin. "I'll fuck you," they said. It sounded to me like, "I'll fix you," and I did not feel broken.

Left: Ivan Albright, *Hail to the Pure.*   **Above:** Julie Foakes, *Untitled.*

I don't believe I've consciously avoided sex. I am always on the verge of wholly giving myself away. I think emotionally, act intuitively. When I'm attracted to someone, I don't hold back. But there have been only a handful of times when I would have gladly had sex. Each, for its own reason, did not happen. I am grateful to have learned so much in the waiting—patience, strength, and ease with solitude.

Do you know what conclusion I've come to? That there is no concrete explanation, and, more important, there doesn't need to be one. How I got here seems less important to me than where I am.

This is what is important. Desire. The circle of my desire widens each day, so that it's no longer contained inside me, but rather, it surrounds me in concentric circles.

Desire overrides everything and should be exploited to its fullest potential. It is the white-hot space between the words. I am desire unfulfilled. I hover over that fiery space feeling the heat without knowing the flames. I am a still life dreaming of animation. I am a bell not allowed to chime. There is a deep stillness inside me. There is a void. A huge part of me is dead to the world, no matter how hard I try to revive it with consoling words or my own brave hand.

I am sick of being sealed up like a grave. I want to be unearthed.

I pray for sex like the pious pray for salvation. I am dying to be physically opened up and exposed. I want to be the source of a man's pleasure. I want to give him that one perfect feeling. I have been my only pleasure for too long.

Do I have dreams about sex? Often. There is one recurring dream in which I can't see whole bodies at once. But I know which parts belong to my body. I know they're mine. I know, better than anyone, my curves, my markings, my sensitive places. If I close my eyes now, I can see the man's body. Thin, smooth, light-haired, limbs spreading and shifting over me like the sea. A small, brick-colored mouth opens and closes around the sphere of a nipple. Moist eyes, the color of darkest honey, roam up and down my spine. A sensation of breath across my belly induces the first wave of moisture between my legs. This reaction crosses the line into wakefulness, and I know when I awaken, the blanket will be twisted aside as if in pain. My skin itself will feel like a fiery blanket, and I will almost feel smothered by it.

In some versions of the dream, I am on top and I can feel my pelvis rubbing against the man's body. Every part of my body is focused on the singular task of getting him inside me. I try and try and am so close, but my fate is that of Tantalus, who was surrounded by water he could not drink. Thank God for masturbation.

My fingers know exactly how to act upon my skin—they have for over half my life now. There is no fear or hesitation. When I masturbate, I am aware of varying degrees of heat throughout my body. It is hottest between my legs. Cool air seems to heat the moment it hits my skin, the moment I suck it in between my lips. After, my hands shake as if I'd had an infusion of caffeine. I press my hand, palm down, in the vale between my breasts, and it feels as if my heart will burst through my hand. I love that feeling—knowing that I'm illimitably alive.

Though I've never had a man inside me, I have had many orgasms. I have talked with girls who not only can't have one with their lover but can't bring themselves to have one. I was shocked at first, until I saw how common it was. And then I felt lucky. My first one scared me. At 12, I did not expect such a reaction to my own touch; I thought I'd hurt myself. But it was such a curious feeling, such a lovely feeling, that I had to explore it further. I felt almost greedy. And, well, I got better at it until it was ridiculously easy. Still, it is always easy.

I don't expect it to be so easy with a man. I've come to believe that sex is defined by affection, not orgasm. There is that need to be held that doesn't disappear when we learn to walk on our own. If anything, it intensifies.

I love being a girl. I think of my body as all scent and soft muscle. It is an imperfect body, but beautiful still in its energy and in its potential. I love looking at my curves in the mirror. I love feeling them and admiring their craftsmanship. I love my hipbones—small, protruding mountains. Or maybe they are like sacred stones marking the entrance to a secret city. I trace the slope of my calf as if it is a slender tree trunk and I am amazed at how strong, yet vulnerable, the human body is. I am as in awe of my body as I am of the earth. My joints are prominent, as if asserting themselves. I know my terrain well, perhaps better than any man ever could—the warm, white softness of my inner arms; the hard, smooth muscle of my bicep like the rounded swelling in a snake that just swallowed the tiniest mouse; the sensitive skin between my thighs; the mole on my pelvis nestled by a vein like a dot on a map marking a city beside a river. I have stared at my naked body in the mirror wondering what the first

I have always believed that our erotic daydreams are the true X-rays of our sexual souls, and like our dreams at night they change as new people and situations enter our lives to be played out against the primitive backdrop of our childhood. An analyst collects his patient's dreams like gold coins. We should value our erotic reveries no less seriously, because they are complex expressions of what we consciously desire and unconsciously fear. To know them is to know ourselves better.

—Nancy Friday

touch from a lover will feel like and where it will be.

Masturbation is pleasurable, but it cannot sustain a whole sexual life. It lacks that vital affection. I am left with the rituals, the mechanics of masturbation. I crash up against the same wall each time. It becomes boring and sad and does little to quell the need to be touched. I long to let go of my body's silent monologue and enter into a dialogue of skin, muscle, and bone.

There are sudden passions that form in my mind when I look at a man. Thoughts of things I want to do to him. I want to follow the veins of his wrists—blue like the heart of a candle flame. I want to lick the depression of his neck as if it were the bottom of a bowl. I want to see the death of my modesty in his eyes. Although I am swollen with romantic ideas, I am not naive. I know it will not be ideal. Rather, it will be bloody, painful, awkward, damp, and dreadful—but that is always the way of birth. It is an act of violence. The threat of pain in pleasure, after all, makes seduction stimulating. I want the pain, to know that I am alive and real—to leave no doubt there has been a transformation.

The fear is undeniable. It's a phobic yearning I have for a man's body, but I have to believe that everything, including fear, is vital when expressing desire. If sexual thoughts are either memories or desires, then I am all desires.

I am powerfully attracted to the male body. I want to watch him undress. See him touch himself. I want his wildness in me—I want to touch his naked body and feel the strength of him. His sweat sliding down the slick surface of my skin until it pools in the crooks of my limbs. I imagine the rhythm of our sex like the slick, undulating motion of swimmers. I imagine my own body's movements suddenly made new, so that we would appear to me like two new bodies. I imagine the sound of our sex—a magnificent, moist clamor of limbs.

I want to hold him inside me like a deep breath. I want to leave kisses as markers on the sharp slices of his shoulder blades, then surrounding the oasis of his belly button. I want to slide him in my mouth like a first taste of wine, letting the bittersweet liquid sweep every part of my mouth before allowing it to slide down my throat.

I will hold my mouth to his ear, as if I were a polished seashell, so he can hear the sea inside me—welcoming him. I will pause and look at him—up into his face. I will steady myself in his gaze, catch the low sun of his cock between my smooth, white thighs, and explode into shine. I will look at him and think, I have spent this man's body and I have spent it well.

Right: Sarah Pletts, *Angus cuddling me.*

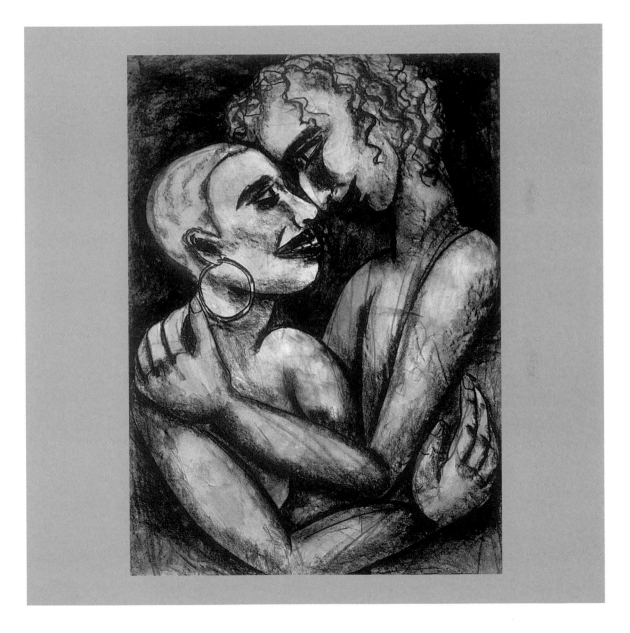

Left: Ivan Albright, *Nude.*

T H I S

Ann Menebroker

You get out of bed
solemnly naked
and lumber somewhere
out of sight.
The house
is a mystery
the way
it swallows
whoever leaves
warm sheets.
Lying here
in my old
bare skin
I think
how I love
the sight

of unclothed people
going about
the business
of love.
Everything else
is so ruined;
the room, the landscape
the world.
The way to stay
beautiful
is to avoid
mirrors
and look only
at those
who truly
love back.

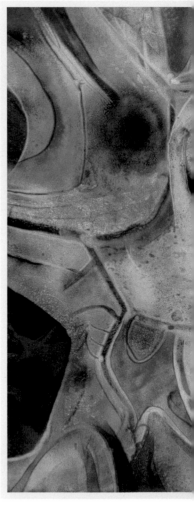

F R O M   T H E   D I A R I E S   O F
A D A M   A N D   E V E

Mark Twain

I FEEL LIKE AN EXPERIMENT, I FEEL EXACTLY LIKE AN EXPERIMENT; IT WOULD BE IMPOSSIBLE for a person to feel more like an experiment than I do, and so I am coming to feel convinced that this is what I am—an experiment; just an experiment, and nothing more . . .

      I followed the other Experiment around, yesterday afternoon, at a distance, to see what it might be for, if I could. But I was not able to make it out. I think it is a man. I had never seen a man, but it looked like one, and I feel sure that

Above: Andrew Lane, *Untitled.* Even in public, couples in love can enter a world where, like Adam and Eve, only the beloved exists. **Right:** Richard Maris Loving, *Untitled.*

that is what it is. I realize that I feel more curiosity about it than about any of the other reptiles. If it is a reptile, and I suppose it is; for it has frowsy hair and blue eyes, and looks like a reptile. It has no hips; it tapers like a carrot; when it stands, it spreads itself apart like a derrick; so I think it is a reptile, though it may be architecture.

I was afraid of it at first, and started to run every time it turned around, for I thought it was going to chase me; but by and by I found it was only trying to get away, so after that I was not timid any more, but tracked it along, several hours, about twenty yards behind, which made it nervous and unhappy. At last it was a good deal worried, and climbed a tree. I waited a good while, then gave it up and went home.

Sunday.—It is up there yet. Resting, apparently. But that is a subterfuge: Sunday isn't the day of rest; Saturday is appointed for that. It looks like a creature that is more interested in resting than in anything else. It would tire me to rest so much. It tires me just to sit around and watch the tree. I do wonder what it is for; I never see it do anything . . .

It has low tastes, and is not kind. When I went there yesterday evening in the gleaming it had crept down and was trying to catch the little speckled fishes that play in the pool, and I had to clod it to make it go up the tree again and let them alone. I wonder if *that* is what it is for? Hasn't it any heart? Hasn't it any compassion for those little creatures? Can it be that it was designed and manufactured for such ungentle work? It has the look of it. One of the clods took it back of the ear, and it used language. It gave me a thrill, for it was the first time I had ever heard speech, except my own. I did not understand the words, but they seemed expressive.

When I found it could talk I felt a new interest in it, for I love to talk; I talk, all day, and in my sleep, too, and I am very interesting, but if I had another to talk to I could be twice as interesting, and would never stop, if desired . . . .

Next week Sunday.—All the week I tagged around after him and tried to get acquainted. I had to do the talking, because he was shy, but I didn't mind it. He seemed pleased to have me around, and I used the sociable "we" a good deal, because it seemed to flatter him to be included.

Wednesday.—We are getting along very well indeed, now, and getting better and better acquainted. He does not try to avoid me any more, which is a good sign, and shows that he likes to have me with him. That pleases me, and I study to be useful to him in every way I can, so as to increase his regard. During the last day or two I have taken all the work of naming things off his hands, and this has been a great relief to him, for he has not gift in that line, and is evidently very grateful. He can't think of a rational name to save him, but I do not let him see that I am aware of his defect. Whenever a new creature comes along I name it before he has time to expose himself by an awkward silence. In this way I have saved him many embarrassments . . .

When the dodo came along he thought it was a wildcat—I saw it in his eye. But I saved him. And I was careful not to do it in a way that could hurt his pride. I just spoke up in a quite natural way of pleased surprise, and not as if I was dreaming of conveying information, and said, "Well, I do declare, if there isn't the dodo!" I explained—without seeming to be explaining—how I knew it for a dodo, and although I thought maybe he was a little piqued that I knew the creature when he didn't, it was quite evident that he admired me. That was very agreeable, and I thought of it once with gratification before I slept. How little a thing can make us happy when we feel that we have earned it!

Adam— *This new creature with the long hair is a good deal in the way. It is always hanging around and following me about. I don't like this; I am not used to company. I wish it would stay with the other animals . . .*

Built me a shelter against the rain, but could not have it to myself in peace. The new creature intruded. When I tried to put it out it shed water out of the holes it looks with, and wiped it away with the back of its paws, and made a noise such as some of the other animals make when they are in distress. I wish it would not talk; it is always talking. that sounds like a cheap fling at the poor creature, a slur; but I do not mean it so. I have never heard the human voice before, and any new and strange sound intruding itself here upon the solemn hush of these dreaming solitudes offends my ear and seems a false note. And this new sound is so close to me; it is right at my shoulder, right at my ear, first on one side and then on the other, and I am used only to sounds that are more or less distant from me . . .

My life is not as happy as it was.

Saturday.—Good deal of fog this morning. I do not go out in the fog myself. The new creature does. It goes out in all weathers, and stumps right in with its muddy feet. And talks. It used to be so pleasant and quiet here . . .

This morning found the new creature trying to clod apples out of that forbidden tree.

Thursday.—My first sorrow. Yesterday he avoided me and seemed to wish I would not talk to him. I could not believe it, and thought this was some mistake, for I loved to be with him, and loved to hear him talk, and so how could it be that he could feel unkind toward me when I had not done anything? But at last it seemed true, so I went away and sat lonely in the place where I first saw him the morning that we were made and I did not know what he was and was indifferent about him; but now it was a mournful place, and every little thing spoke of him, and my heart was very sore. I did not know why very clearly, for it was a new feeling; I had not experienced it before, and it was all a mystery, and I could not make it out.

But when night came I could not bear the lonesomeness, and went to the new shelter which he has built, to ask him what I had done that was wrong and how I could mend it and get back his kindness again; but he put me out in the rain, and it was my first sorrow.

Sunday.—It is pleasant again, now, and I am happy; but those were heavy days; I do not think of them when I can help it.

I tried to get him some of those apples, but I cannot learn to throw straight. I failed, but I think the good intention pleased him. They are forbidden, and he says I shall come to harm . . .

Monday.—This morning I told him my name, hoping it would interest him. But he did not care for it. It is strange. If he should tell me his name, I would care. I think it would be pleasanter in my ears than any other sound.

He talks very little. Perhaps it is because he is not bright, and is sensitive about it and wishes to conceal it. It is such a pity that he should feel so, for brightness is nothing; it is in the heart that the values lie. I wish I could make him understand that a loving good heart is riches, and riches enough, and that without it intellect is poverty.

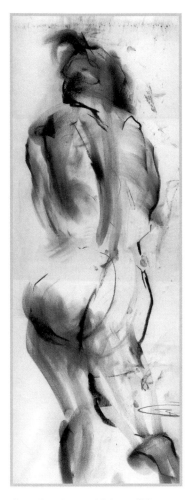

Above: Barry Peterson, *II-Gesture #10*

Adam—   The new creature says its name is Eve . . . It says it is not an It, it is a She.

Tuesday.—All the morning I was at work improving the estate; and I purposely kept away from him in the hope that he would get lonely and come. But he did not.

At noon I stopped for the day and took my recreation by flitting all about with the bees and the butterflies and reveling in the flowers, those beautiful creatures that catch the smile of God out of the sky and preserve it! I gathered them, and made them into wreaths and garlands and clothed myself in them while I ate my luncheon—apples, of course; then I sat in the shade and wished and waited. But he did not come.

But no matter. Nothing would have come of it, for he does not care for flowers. He calls them rubbish, and cannot tell one from another, and thinks it is superior to feel like that. He does not care for me, he does not care for flowers, he does not care for the painted sky at eventide—is there anything he does care for, except building shacks to coop himself up in from the good clean rain, and thumping the melons, and sampling the grapes, and fingering the fruit on the trees, to see how those properties are coming along?

Adam—   She has been climbing that tree again. Clodded her out of it. She said nobody was looking. Seems to consider that a sufficient justification for chancing any dangerous thing. Told her that. The word justification moved her admiration—and envy, too, I thought. It is a good word.

Tuesday.—She told me she was made out of a rib taken from my body. This is at least doubtful, if not more than that. I have not missed any rib.

Sunday.—Pulled through.

She has ten up with a snake now. The other animals are glad, for she was always experimenting with them and bothering them; and I am glad because the snake talks, and this enables me to get a rest.

Friday.—She says the snake advises her to try the fruit of that tree, and says the result will be a great and fine and noble education . . . . I advised her to keep away from the tree. She said she wouldn't. I foresee trouble.

Perhaps I ought to remember that she is very young, a mere girl, and make allowances. She is all interest, eagerness, vivacity; the world is to her a charm, a wonder, a mystery, a joy; she can't speak for delight when she a new flower, she must pet it and caress it and smell it and talk to it, and pour out endearing names upon it. And she is color-mad: brown rocks, yellow sand, gray moss, green foliage, blue sky; the pearl of the dawn, the purple shadows on the mountains, the golden islands floating in crimson seas at sunset, the pallid moon sailing through the shredded cloud-rack, the star-jewels glittering in the wastes of space—none of them is of any practical value, so far as I can see, but because they have color and majesty, that is enough for her, and she loses her mind over them. If she could quiet down and keep still a couple of minutes at a time, it would be a reposeful spectacle. In that case I think I could enjoy looking at her; indeed I am sure I could, for I am coming to realize that she is a quite remarkably comely creature—lithe, slender, trim, rounded, shapely, nimble, graceful; and once when she was standing marble-white and sun-drenched on a boulder, with her young head tilted back and her hand shading her eyes, watching the flight of a bird in the sky, I recognized that she was beautiful.

Monday noon.—If there is anything on the planet that she is not interested in it is not in my list. There are animals that I am indifferent to, but it is not so with her. She has no discrimination, she takes to all of them, she thinks they are all treasures, every new one is welcome.

When the mighty brontosaurus came striding into camp, she regarded it as an acquisition, I considered it a calamity; that is a good example of the lack of harmony that prevails in our views of things. She wanted to domesticate it, I wanted to make it a present of the homestead and move out. She believed it could be tamed by kind treatment and would be a good pet; I said a pet twenty-feet high and eighty-four feet long would be no proper thing to have about the place, because, even with the best intentions and without meaning any harm, it could sit down on the house and mash it, for anyone could see by the look of its eye that it was absent-minded.

Still, her heart was set upon having that monster, and she couldn't give it up. She thought we could start a dairy with it, and wanted me to help her milk it; but I wouldn't; it was too risky. The sex wasn't right, and we hadn't any ladder anyway. Then she wanted to ride it, and look at the scenery. Thirty or forty feet of its tail was lying on the ground, like a fallen tree, and she thought she could climb it, but she was mistaken, when she got to the steep place it was too slick and down she came, and would have hurt herself but for me.

Was she satisfied now? No. Nothing ever satisfies her but demonstration; untested theories are not in her line, and she won't have them. It is the right spirit, I concede it; it attracts me; I feel the influence of it; if I were with her more I think I should take it up myself. Well, she had one theory remaining about this colossus: she thought that if we could tame him and make him friendly we could stand him in the river and use him for a bridge. It turned out that he was already plenty tame enough—at least as far as she was concerned—so she tried her theory, but it failed: every time she got him properly placed in the river and went ashore to cross over on him, he came out and followed her around like a pet mountain. Like the other animals. They all do that.

Above: An illustration by Margaret C. Cook for Whitman's, *Leaves of Grass.*

Friday—Tuesday—Wednesday—Thursday-and to-day: all without seeing him. It is a long time to be alone; still, it is better to be alone than unwelcome.

I *had* to have company I was made for it, I think—so I made friends with the animals. They are just charming, and they have the kindest disposition and the politest ways; they never look sour, they never let you feel that you are intruding, they smile at you and wag their tail, if they've got one, and they are always ready for a romp or an excursion or anything you want to propose. I think they are perfect gentlemen. All these days we have had such good times, and it hasn't been lonesome for me, ever . . .

The birds and animals are all friendly to each other, and there are no disputes about anything. They all talk, and they all talk to me, but it must be a foreign language, for I cannot make out a word they say; yet they often understand me when I talk back, particularly the dog and the elephant. It makes me ashamed. It shows that they are brighter than I am, and are therefore my superiors. It annoys me, for I want to be the principal Experiment myself—and I intend to be, too.

To love another person is to see the face of God.

—Victor Hugo

a f t e r   t h e   f a l l

When I look back, the Garden is a dream to me. It was beautiful, surpassingly beautiful, enchantingly beautiful; and now it is lost, and I shall not see it any more.

The Garden is lost, but I have found *him,* and am content. He loves me as well as he can; I love him with all the strength of my passionate nature, and this, I think, is proper to my youth and sex. If I ask myself why I love him, I find I do not know, and do not really much care to know; so I suppose that this kind of love is not a product of reasoning and statistics, like one's love for other reptiles and animals. I think that this must be so. I love certain birds because of their song; but I do not love Adam on account of his singing—no, it is not that; the more he sings the more I do not get reconciled to it. Yet I ask him to sing, because I wish to learn to like everything he is interested in. I am sure I can learn, because at first I could not stand it, but now I can. It sours the milk, but it doesn't matter; I can get used to that kind of milk.

It is not on account of his brightness that I love him—no, it is not that. He is not to blame for his brightness, such as it is, for he did not make it himself; he is as God made him, and that is sufficient. There was a wise purpose in it, *that* I know. In time it will develop, though I think it will not be sudden; and besides, there is no hurry; he is well enough just as he is.

It is not on account of his gracious and considerate ways and his delicacy that I love him. No, he has lacks in these regards, but he is well enough just so, and is improving.

It is not on account of his industry that I love him—no, it is not that. I think he has it in him, and I do not know why he conceals it from me. It is my only pain. Otherwise he is frank and open with me, now . . .

Then why is it that I love him? *Merely because he is masculine,* I think.

At bottom he is good, and I love him for that, but I could love him without it. If he should beat me and abuse me, I should go on loving him. I know it. It is a matter of sex, I think.

He is strong and handsome, and I love him for that, and I admire him and am proud of him, but I could love him without those qualities. If he were plain, I should love him; if he were a wreck, I should love him; and I would work for him, and slave over him, and pray for him, and watch by his bedside until I died.

Yes, I think I love him merely because he is *mine* and is *masculine.* There is no other reason, I suppose. . . . It just comes—none knows whence—and cannot explain itself. And doesn't need to.

It is what I think. But I am only a girl, and the first that has examined this matter, and it may turn out that in my ignorance and inexperience I have not got it right.

f o r t y   y e a r s   l a t e r

After all these years, I see that I was mistaken about Eve in the beginning; it is better to live outside the Garden with her than inside it without her. At first I thought she talked too much; but now I should be sorry to have that voice fall silent and pass out of my life . . . [She] has taught me to know the goodness of her heart and the sweetness of her spirit!

It is my prayer, it is my longing, that we may pass from this life together—a longing which shall never perish from the earth, but shall have place in the heart of every wife that loves, until the end of time; and it shall be called by my name.

But if one of us must go first, it is my prayer that it shall be I; for he is strong, I am weak, I am not so necessary to him as he is to me—life without him would not be life; how could I endure it? This prayer is also immortal, and will not cease from being offered up while my race continues. I am the first wife; and in the last wife I shall be repeated.

a t   e v e ' s   g r a v e

Adam—   Wheresoever she was, there was Eden.

Left: For a woman to be a fox means being both sexy and knowing, here epitomized by screen legend, Mae West, circa 1935.

E V E T H E F O X

Paula Gunn Allen

EVE THE FOX SWUNG
her hips appetizingly, she
sauntered over to Adam the hunk
who was twiddling his toes and
devising an elaborate scheme
for renaming the beasts: Adam
was bored, but not Eve for she
knew the joy of swivelhips
and the taste of a honey on her lips.
She was serpent wise and snake foolish,
and she knew all the tricks of the trade
that foxy lady, and she used them
to wile away the time: bite into this,
my hunky mate, she said, bending
tantalizingly low so her warm breasts
hung like ripe peaches from a bough. You
will know a thing or two when I get
through to you, she said, and gazed
deep with promise into his dazzled eyes.

She admired the glisten of sweat and light
on his muscled arms, that hunky man of mine,
she sighed inside and wiggled deliciously
while he bit deep into the golden fruit
she held to his lips. And wham-bam,
the change arose, it rose up in Adam
as it had in Eve, and let me tell you
right then they knew all
they ever wanted to know about knowing,
And he discovered the perfect curve of her
breasts, the sweet gentle halfmoon of her belly,
the perfect valentine of her vulva,
the rose that curled within the garden
of her loins that he would enter like bees.
And she discovered the tender power
of his sweat, the strong center of his
arms, she worshiped his dark hair
that fell over her face and arms like the sea.
And together riding the current of this
altogether new knowing they had found.
They bit and chewed, bit and chewed.

THE DATE

Brenda Miller

When I return naked to the stone porch,
there is no one to see me glistening.
—Linda Gregg

A MAN I LIKE IS COMING FOR DINNER TONIGHT. THIS MEANS I DON'T SLEEP VERY MUCH, and I wake up at dawn, disoriented, wondering where I am. I look at my naked body stretched diagonally across the bed; I look at the untouched breasts, the white belly, and I wonder. I don't know if this man will ever touch me, but I wonder.

I get up, and I make coffee. While I wait for the water to boil I vaguely study the pictures and poems and quotes held in place by magnets on my refrigerator. I haven't really looked at these things in a long time, my gaze usually blinking out as I reach for the refrigerator door. This morning I try to look at these objects clearly, objectively, as if I were a stranger, trying to figure what this man will think of them and so, by extension, what he will make of me.

He'll see pictures of my three nieces, my nephew, my godson. He'll see my six women friends hiking in a slot canyon of the San Rafael swell, straddling the narrow gap

Left: Greta Garbo, Swedish-American film actress in MGM's *Romance*, 1932. Definitely dressed to go somewhere special.

with their strong thighs, their muscular arms. He'll see the astrological forecast for Pisces ("There's never been a better moment to turn your paranoia into *pronoia*," it insists), and the Richard Campbell quote which tells me if I'm to live like a hero I must be ready at any moment, "there is no other way." He'll see Rumi "Let the Beauty we love be what we do. There are hundreds of ways to kneel and kiss the ground." He'll see me kayaking with my friend Kathy in the San Juan Islands, and then, if his gaze moves in a clockwise direction, he'll see me standing on the estate of Edna St. Vincent Millay, my arms around my fellow artist colonists, grinning as if I were genuinely happy.

Who is this person on my refrigerator door? Every morning, these bits and pixels try to coalesce into a coherent image, a picture by which to navigate as I move solitary through my morning routine of coffee, juice, cereal. I suppose we attach these things to our refrigerators as subliminal reminders of self, but I've seen these fragments so often they've come to mean nothing to me. I know this collage exists only for others, a constructed persona for the few people who make it this far into my house, my kitchen, my life. Look, it says, look how (athletic, spiritual, creative, loved) I am. And my impulse, though I stifle it, is to rearrange all these items: delete some, add others, in order to create a picture I think this man will like.

But how could I know? How would I keep from making a mistake? Besides, I tell myself, a mature woman would never perform such a silly and demeaning act. So I turn away from the fridge, leave things the way they are. I drink my coffee and gaze out the window. It's February, and the elm trees are bare, the grass brown under patches of snow. Tomorrow is Valentine's Day, a fact I've been avoiding. I think about the blue tulips I planted in the fall, still hunkered underground, and the thought of them in the darkness, their pale shoots nudging the hard-packed soil, makes me a little afraid.

I'm afraid because I'm 38 years old, and I've been alone for almost three years now, have dated no one since leaving my last boyfriend, who is now marrying someone else in California. Sometimes I like to be alone; I come into my bedroom, pleased by the polish of light through the half-closed Venetian blinds. I lie on my bed at odd hours of the day with a small lavender pillow over my eyes, like the old woman I think I'm becoming. At times like these, the light in my bedroom seems a human thing, kind and forgiving, and my solitude a position to be envied, guarded, even if it means I will remain unpartnered for life.

But this feeling of "unpartneredness" can also set me adrift. Sometimes I can't move beyond the threshold of my bedroom door; I stand there, paralyzed, panic scrabbling beneath my skin. I try to breathe deeply, try to remember the smiling self on my refrigerator door, but that person seems all surface, a lie rehearsed so many times it bears a faint semblance to truth. I cry as if every love I've known has been false somehow, a trick. This subliminal loneliness seems more real, more true somehow, than any transient moments of happiness.

At these times I want only to be part of the coupled universe, attached to some cornice which might solidify my presence in a world which too often renders me invisible. In my parents' house an entire wall is devoted to formal family photographs, and the family groupings fall into neat, symmetrical lines: my older brother, his wife and two children flanking one side of my parents; my younger brother, his wife and two children balance out the other. When I lived with my boyfriend Keith for five years, my parents insisted we take a portrait as well, and we did: me in a green T-shirt and multicolored beads, Keith in jeans and a denim shirt, standing with our arms entwined. So for a while, my photo, and my life, fit neatly into the familial constellation.

Keith and I split up, but the photo remained on the wall a year longer, staring down at me when I came to visit for Hanukkah. "You have to take that down," I finally told them, and they nodded sadly, said "we know." Now a portrait of myself, alone, hangs in its place—a nice photograph, flattering, but it still looks out of line amid the growing and changing families that surround it. Whenever I visit, my 8-year-old nephew asks me, "Why aren't you married?" and gazes at me with a mixture of wonder and alarm.

A man I like is coming to dinner and so I get out all my cookbooks and choose and discard recipes as if trying on dresses. I want something savory yet subtle, not too garlicky, just in case we kiss. I don't know if we'll kiss, but just in case. I think about condoms, and blush, and wonder if he will buy any, wonder where they are in the store, how much they cost these days. I wonder about the weight of a man's hands on my shoulders, on my hair. Marilyn Robinson, in *Housekeeping,* writes that "need can blossom into all the compensations it requires . . . . To wish for a hand on one's hair is all but to feel it. So whatever we may lose, very craving gives it back to us again."

I want to believe her, so I crave the hand. I close my eyes and try to picture this man's wrists, to feel the soft underside of his wrist against my mouth. And yes, I feel it. Yes, my breath catches in my throat, as if he stroked his thumb against the edge of my jaw. My body's been so long without desire I've almost forgotten what it means to be a sexual being, to feel this quickening in my groin. And it's all I need for now: this moment of desire unencumbered by the complications of fulfillment. Because craving only gives rise to more craving; desire feeds on itself, and cannot be appeased. It is *my* desire after all, *my* longing, more delicious than realization, because over this longing I retain complete control.

It will be our third date, this dinner. From what I've heard, the third date's either the charm or the poison. I have a friend who in the last five years has never "gotten past the third date." She calls me at 10:30 on a Friday night. "Third date syndrome," she sighs. She describes the sheepish look on her date's face as she returns to the table after a trip to the ladies room. She tells me about the "let's just be friends speech" that by now she has memorized: "You're great. I enjoy your company, but a) I don't have a lot of time right now, b) I'm not looking for a relationship, c) I'm going to be out of town a lot in the next couple of months." My friend sighs and tells me: "I just wish one of them would come right out and say, 'Look, I don't really like you. Let's just forget it.' It would be a relief."

When we hang up I turn back to my empty house, the bed whose wide expanse looks accusatory in my bedside light, the pile of books that has grown lopsided and dangerous. I stare at my fish, a fighting fish named Betty, who flares his gills at me and swims in vicious circles around his plastic hexagon, whips his iridescent body back and forth. My friend Connie tells me this behavior indicates love, that my fish is expressing his masculinity so I might want to mate with him. It's a sign of my desperation that I take this explanation as a compliment.

I lied. I changed everything on my refrigerator, on my bulletin board, on my mantelpiece. I casually put up a picture, half-hidden, of myself on a good day, my tan legs long, my skin flawless as I pose in front of a blazing maple bush on Mill Creek. I try to suppress an unbidden fantasy: a photograph of me and this man and his two daughters filling in the empty place on my parents' wall. Yesterday I discussed this imminent dinner with my hairstylist, Tony, as he bobbed my hair. Tony is my guru. When I came to him the first time, I told him my hair was in a transition: not long, not short, just annoying. "You can't think of it," said Tony, cupping my unwanted flip, "as a transition. This is what your hair wants to be right now. There are no transitions. This is *it,* right now."

Yesterday, he cupped my newly-coifed hair in his slender fingers, gazed at me somberly in the mirror. I smiled uncertainly, cocked my head. "Good?" he asked.

"Good," I replied. He whisked bits of hair off my shoulders with a stiff brush. "Don't worry," he said. "Play it cool." I nodded, gazing at myself in the mirror which always makes my cheeks look a little too pudgy, my lips too pale. Whenever I look at myself too long, I become unrecognizable, my mouth slightly askew, a mouth I can't imagine kissing or being kissed. I paid Tony, then walked carefully out of the salon, my head level, a cold breeze against my bare neck. In the car, I did not resist the urge to pull down the rear view mirror and look at myself again. I touched my new hair. I touched those lips, softly, with the very tips of my fingers.

A man I like is coming to dinner. In two hours. The chicken is marinating, and the house is clean and if I take a shower now and get dressed I'll have an hour and a half to sit fidgeting on my living room chair, talking to myself and to the fish, whose water, of course I've changed. "Make a good impression," I plead with him. "Mellow out." He swims back and forth, avoiding my eyes, butting his pinhead against the plastic hexagon.

A date. The word still brings up visions of Solvang, California and the date orchards on the outskirts of town, the sticky sweetness of the dark fruit. We drove through the orchards on car trips during the summers, my family hot and irritable in the blue station wagon. But when we stopped at the stores which had giant dates painted on awnings we grew excited, our misery forgotten. My mother doled the fruit out to us from the front seat, her eyes already half-closed in pleasure. The dates—heavy, cloying, dark as dried blood—always made the roof of my mouth itch, but I ate them anyway because they came in a white box like candy. I ate them because I was told they were precious, the food of the gods.

A man I like is coming to dinner. He's late. I sit on the edge of my bed, unwilling to stand near the front windows where he might see me waiting. My stomach hurts, and is not soothed by the smell of Tandoori chicken overcooking in the oven. My hands, like a cliché, are sweating. I lie back on the bed, at this point not caring if I mess up my hair, or wrinkle my green dress chosen for its apparent lack of effort. My name is painted in Japanese above my black bureau. Pieces of myself are scattered all around me: a blue kilim from Turkey, a seashell from Whidbey Island, a candlestick from Portugal. Pale light sifts through the Venetian blinds at an angle just right for napping or making love. If I had to choose right now, I'd choose a nap, the kind that keeps me hovering on the edge of a consciousness so sweet it would seem ridiculous to ever resurface. My lavender eye pillow is within reach. My house is so small; how could it possibly accommodate a man, filling my kitchen chairs, peering at my refrigerator door?

On my bedside table is *The Pillow Book* of Sei Shonagan, a Japanese courtesan of the 10th century, a woman whose career consisted in waiting. In this expectant state, she observed everything around her in great detail, found some of it to her liking and some not. I idly pick the book up and allow it to fall open. I read, "When a woman lives alone, her house should be extremely dilapidated, the mud wall should be falling to pieces, and if there is a pond, it should be overgrown with water plants. It is not essential that the garden be covered with sage-brush; but weeds should be growing through the sand in patches, for this gives the place a poignantly desolate look."

I close the book. I look around this apartment, this house where I live alone. My room feels clean, new, expectant. Now I want nothing more than to stay alone, to hold myself here in a state of controlled desire. But if this man doesn't show, I know my house will quickly settle into the dilapidation Shonagan saw fit for a single woman; the line between repose and chaos is thinner than I once thought.

The doorbell rings, startling me into a sitting position. I clear my throat, which suddenly seems ready to close altogether, to keep me mute and safe. I briefly consider leaving the door unanswered; I imagine my date waiting, looking through the kitchen window, then backing away and into his car, shaking his head, wondering. Perhaps he would think me crazy, or dead. Perhaps he would call the police, tell them there's a woman he's worried about, a woman who lives alone. Or, more likely, he would drive to a bar, have a beer, forget about me. The thought of his absence momentarily pleases me, bathes me with relief. But of course I stand up and glance in the mirror, rake my hands through my hair to see it feather into place, and casually walk out to greet this man I like, this man who's coming to dinner.

Right: The perennial lure of romance used in advertising.

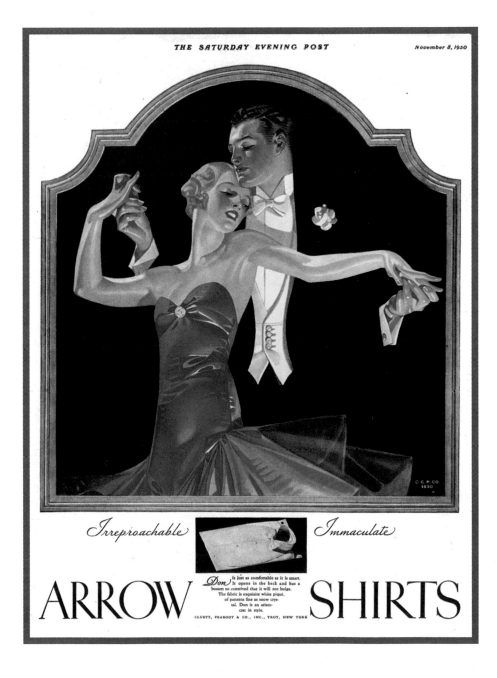

S L E E P Y   T I M E   G A L

Gary Gildner

I N THE SMALL TOWN IN NORTHERN MICHIGAN WHERE MY FATHER lived as a young man, he had an Italian friend who worked in a restaurant. I will call his friend Phil. Phil's job in the restaurant was as ordinary as you can imagine—from making coffee in the morning to sweeping up at night. But what was not ordinary about Phil was his piano playing. On Saturday nights my father and Phil and their girlfriends would drive ten or fifteen miles to a roadhouse by a lake where they would drink beer from schoopers and dance and Phil would play an old beat-up piano. He could play any song you named, my father said, but the song everyone waited for was the one he wrote, which he would always play at the end before they left to go back to the town. And everyone knew of course that he had written the song for his girl, who was as pretty as she was rich. Her father was the banker in their town, and he was a tough old German, and he didn't like Phil going around with his daughter.

Left: Famous songster, Neil Sedaka.   **Right:** A valentine card from 1911. Love or dollars? Love bids you make a choice!

My father, when he told the story, which was not often, would tell it in an offhand way and emphasize the Depression and not having much, instead of the important parts. I will try to tell it the way he did, if I can.

So they would go to the roadhouse by the lake, and finally Phil would play his song, and everyone would say, Phil, that's a great song, you could make a lot of money from it. But Phil would only shake his head and smile and look at his girl. I have to break in here and say that my father, a gentle but practical man, was not inclined to emphasize the part about Phil looking at his girl. It was my mother who said the girl would rest her head on Phil's shoulder while he played, and that he got the idea for the song from the pretty way she looked when she got sleepy. My mother was not part of the story, but she had heard it when she and my father were younger and therefore had that information. I would like to intrude further and add something about Phil writing the song, maybe show him whistling the tune and going over the words slowly and carefully to get the best ones, while peeling onions or potatoes in the restaurant; but my father is already driving them home from the roadhouse, and saying how patched up his tires were, and how his car's engine was a gingerbread of parts from different makes, and some parts were his own invention as well. And my mother is saying that the old German had made his daughter promise not to get involved with any man until after college, and they couldn't be late. Also my mother likes the sad parts and is eager to get to their last night before the girl goes away to college.

So they all went out to the roadhouse, and it was sad. The women got tears in their eyes when Phil played her song, my mother said. My father said that Phil spent his week's pay on a new shirt and tie, the first tie he ever owned, and people kidded him. Somebody piped up and said, Phil, you ought to take that song down to Bay City—which was like saying New York City to them, only more realistic—and sell it and take the money and go to college too. Which was not meant to be cruel, but that was the result because Phil had never even got to high school. But you can see people were trying to cheer him up, my mother said.

Well, she'd come home for Thanksgiving and Christmas and Easter and they'd all sneak out to the roadhouse and drink beer from schoopers and dance and everything would be like always. And of course there were the summers. And everyone knew Phil and the girl would get married after she made good her promise to her father because you could see it in their eyes when he sat at the old beat-up piano and played her song.

That last part about their eyes was not, of course, in my father's telling, but I couldn't help putting it in there even though I know it is making some of you impatient. Remember that this happened many years ago in the woods by a lake in northern Michigan, before television. I wish I could put more in, especially about the song and how it felt to Phil to sing it and how the girl felt when hearing it and knowing it was hers, but I've already intruded too much in a simple story that isn't even mine.

Well, here's the kicker part. Probably by now many of you have guessed that one vacation near the end she doesn't come home to see Phil, because she meets some guy at college who is good-looking and as rich as she is and, because her father knew about Phil all along and was pressuring her into forgetting about him, she gives in to this new guy and goes to his hometown during the vacation and falls in love with him. That's how the people in town figured it, because after she graduates they turn up, already married, and right away he takes over the old German's bank—and buys a new Pontiac at the place where my father is the mechanic and pays cash for it. The paying cash always made my father pause and shake his head and mention again that times were tough, but here comes this guy in a spiffy white shirt (with French cuffs, my mother said) and pays the full price in cash.

And this made my father shake his head too: Phil took the song down to Bay City and sold it for twenty-five dollars, the only money he ever got for it. It was the same song we'd just heard on the radio and which reminded my father of the story I just told you. What happened to Phil? Well, he stayed in Bay City and got a job managing a movie theater. My father saw him there after the Depression when he was on his way to Detroit to work for Ford. He stopped and Phil gave him a box of popcorn. The song he wrote for the girl has sold many millions of records, and if I told you the name of it you could probably sing it, or at least whistle the tune. I wonder what the girl thinks when she hears it. Oh yes, my father met Phil's wife too. She worked in the movie theater with him, selling tickets and cleaning the carpet after the show with one of those sweepers you push. She was also big and loud and nothing like the other one, my mother said.

W I L D   N I G H T S — W I L D   N I G H T S

Emily Dickinson

WILD NIGHTS—WILD NIGHTS!
Were I with thee
Wild Nights should be
Our luxury!

Futile— the Winds—
To a Heart In port—
Done with the Compass—
Done with the Chart!

Right: In his heyday, Italian-born actor Rudolph Valentino was a heartthrob with a wild and dangerous sexuality.

T H E   K I S S

William Sansom

As Rolfe began to lean over her, knowing the moment had come, he understood for the first time the meaning of isolation. On the very brink of it he was separated from her suddenly by a grim and cold distance along whose way could he detected the chill of reality.

She lay back in the cushions, her hair loose on the taffeta, her lips parted in a smile of invitation. The pink tip of her tongue lingered between her teeth. In that hot weather there were night-flies, and away by the lamp one of these hummed through the stillness of an apprehensive room. Only once was this silence, the silence of the dynamo, disturbed—when the girl raised her arms towards his, when the taffeta cushions rustled and the starched crinkle of her silken dress livened the air with whispers that seemed to mould musically the shape of her own delighted motion.

Why should he have felt at that time so separate, more separated from her than ever before. More even than at their first strange meeting? In the wisp of time when his lips approached hers—even then!—he sought wildly for the reason. Perhaps he had flung himself back the better to leap forward, recoiling instinctively for the assault? Perhaps he was afraid of refusal, so that in his wounded pride the hate had already begun to crystallize? Perhaps he was certain of acceptance; and thus with the knowledge of conquest saturating his hope, he was already reaching out for another star, belittling the planet whose illusory brilliance had faded in the shadow of his near approach. All these three emotions had a part in him, then, but the last predominated.

Yet—whatever the mind said, the lips and the instincts were already on the move. Wherever hope had flown, desire was gathering momentum; desire must be consuaged. Now it seemed to freewheel—like the gilded mountain train that had strained so desperately towards the summit, with pistons boiling, with each socket shuddering in a cloud of steam and smoke and noise, only to reach the top, pause and then run coolly into its descent, freewheeling with relief, sure of its rails and its effortless glide down to an inevitable destination below. How simple it seemed! Yet that was only the beginning.

For as his head bent lower the idea of conquest became an idea of possession. Still from a distance, but nearer, so much nearer, he saw his love as he wished her to be. He saw the curve of her bare shoulder shining whitely even in the pink glow of the shaded gaslight. He saw how the shoulder was thrust towards him, so that her cheek nestled against it, her head thrust a little to one side, not coquettish, but thoughtful, as though she were considering carefully and with deep satisfaction on the beloved moment and the fulfillment that lay at its end. Her eyes half-closed, so that under dark brows their blue gleamed cloudily between lids heavy with the night's honey. And one strand of her hair blew free across her cheek, touching the corner of her mouth. She smiled lazily, with teeth so slightly parted, the smile of one awakening from the warmth of sleep. At the collar of her dress an ivory locket breathed quickly and lightly. He repeated and repeated to himself: "This is mine! This is all mine to kiss!" This is the property of that stranger I call myself, whom I have watched growing, whom I have applauded and despised, whom

There are wild, hungry kisses or there are rollicking kisses, and there are kisses fluttery and soft as the feathers of cockatoos. It's as if, in the complex language of love, there were a word that could only be spoken by lips when lips touch, a silent contract sealed with a kiss.

—Diane Ackerman

once I saw as a little boy breaking his nails on a walnut shell, running to his mother, carrying a prize off the school platform with violent self-satisfaction: and as a young man miserable in the first secrecies of love, walking cleverly to the office, always seeing himself as a different person much older; and now as a man whose ambitions are outlined, who has failed often, but who has known small successes too, and feels them rise into a tide of achievement. And now—once more a moment of success, the greatest yet! The stranger has achieved the ability to kiss this lovely and fabulous creature, so recently held to be far beyond his feeble reach! The stranger has exerted his charms and he has won, so that now the treasure lies at his feet, and he himself stands above that which was once considered too high for him.

Shall the stranger now brush this treasure aside with his boots?

Not on his life! For the momentum of desire is piling up its swift descent, Rolfe's head is bending lower, the lips are forming themselves into the framework of a kiss. Besides, vanity is not the only emotion that stirs the stranger's heart; he begins as well to appreciate purely and profoundly the loveliness that lies before him.

As Rolfe bends forward, the room around departs, his eyes focus only on the figure in the light beneath, and then softly over this vision creeps a sentimental mist that suffuses the hair, the eyes, the lips, the face with a luster of even great beauty, as though a halo has been thrown around it and over it, as though it were a face seen through tears. A wishful sob mounts in his throat. Her hands touch his shoulders.

But—even then he is distracted. At one side of the halo a golden tassel shines in the light. Somehow, although he is looking directly down into her face, the corner of his eye manages to digest the fact of this golden tassel. In an instant his mind has traveled all the way to a theatre curtain, a stage, a particular play, and a tired quarrel afterwards in a drawing-room where there was no fire and the sandwiches were bent and stale.

Then his eyes advance, so that the tassel is lost in the gray mists that circle his vision, departing as suddenly as it had arrived, leaving no impression at all.

His eyes are so near to her face that suddenly he can see everything! He can see clearly, as though through an optical glass, the lowered lids with their rim of blue mascara, the pubic tenderness of the hairs at her brow, the mineral luster of the greasepaint that makes a black beauty spot of the brown mole on her cheek. Her lips are filmed with wetness through which he can see the dry rouge. There is a tiny bubble of saliva between two teeth. He notices that there are larger pores on the sides of her nostrils, and that the powder has caked beneath them. She has a mustache! But how fine, how sweet, a mirage of the softest down!

And now truly love sweeps over him. For he loves all these things, their nearness, their revelation, their innocent nudity offered without care. He loves it that beneath the perfect vision there lie these pathetic and human strugglings. The vision has become a person. He has at last penetrated beneath the cloak of the perfume and smells at last the salt that breathes closest to her skin. This is a magic moment when ambitions are more than realized, even before they are tasted! For now the moment of fulfillment is so very close that the urgency of desire's speed seems to vanish. There is a second of leisure, a last fondling of the object soon to be grasped—that will never recur. Perhaps the only real moment of possession, the moment just before possession, when desire knows that there is no longer even the necessity to freewheel. Can there be such a pause in the great momentum? It must be so. Just as the mountain train having completed the swift gradient runs for the last lap once more on level rails, slowing without effort its speed, but never doubting that it will glide surely to its final rest at the buffers.

        Their eyes closed. With parted lips they kissed. He opened his eyes, so slightly, to look once more at the face he loved. An agony clutched his spine! He saw with terror that her eyes were wide open, wide and blue, staring at the ceiling! Heavens—had they ever closed? Had they opened at the very moment that their lips had touched? Had she remained unkissed? Had she never kissed him? Would he ever know? How could he trust her answer—perhaps that her dress had caught, or that her eyes were open in a dream? Were these eyes blind with the distances of passion, or were they alert with thought? And what thought? How could he ever know? Even as he tried to solve them her eyes turned from above and stared straight into his.

Right: Andrew Lane, *Beauty is in the Eye of the Beholder.*

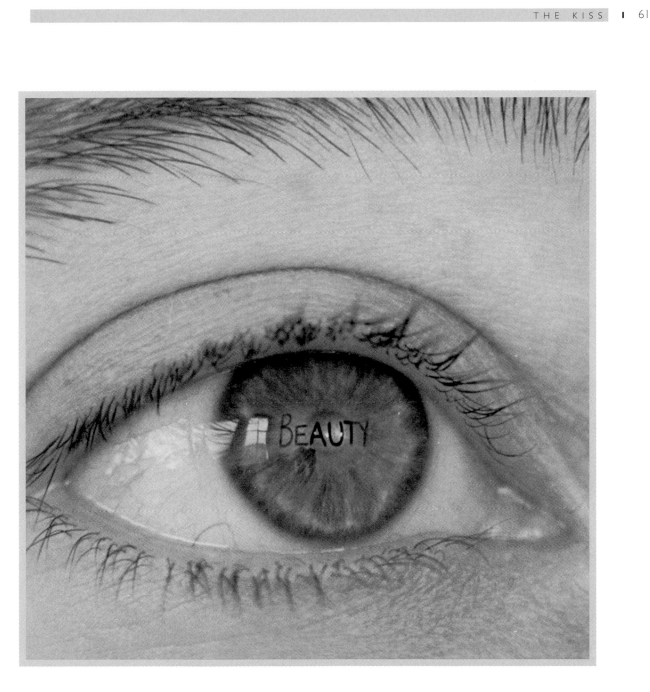

EXCERPT FROM THE SONG OF SONGS

From *The Old Testament*

LIKE AN APPLE TREE AMONG THE
Trees of the forest
Is my lover among the young men.
I delight to sit in his shade,
And his fruit is sweet to my taste.
He has taken me to the banquet hall,
And his banner over me is love.
Strengthen me with raisins,
Refresh me with apples,
For I am faint with love.

His left arm is under my head,
And his right arm embraces me.
Daughters of Jerusalem, I charge you,
By the gazelles and by the does in the field:
Do not arouse or awaken love
Until it so desires.

Listen! My lover!
Look! Here he comes,
Leaping across the mountains,
Bounding over the hills.
My lover is like a gazelle or a young stag,
Look! There he stands behind our wall,
Gazing through the windows,
Peering through the lattice.
My lover spoke and said to me,
"Arise my darling,
my beautiful one, and come with me.
See! The winter is past;
The rains are over and gone.
Flowers appear on the earth:
The season of singing has come,
The cooing of doves is heard in our land.
The fig tree forms its early fruit;
The blossoming vines spread their fragrance.
Arise, come, my darling:
My beautiful one, come with me.

Left: Louis Barlow, *Jitterbugs.* The dancers in the picture show a joyous abandon echoed in the text.

A F O U R T H O F J U L Y

Joe Balay

ABOUT A WEEK AFTER RAYNARD JOHNSON'S BODY WAS FOUND HANGING IN A pecan tree down in mississippi, and just a few days before the government failed a missile test in outerspace that made the sky look like it was giving birth, my girlfriend called to tell me she was house-sitting for her uncle. it was the same day that a little more than two hundred years ago america claimed its independence by killing some englishmen on the cast coast, and i am hungover.

. . .

a half hour passes and i make a left onto a small inarticulate road that leads into a silicon valley. on either side of the road there are distinguished houses, two stories, dull, and either grey or blue.sarah meets me in a bikini in front of the house and she is sunbathing. i hate the sun.

. . .

all day long we sit around a swimming pool and a playground and a cactus garden pretending to belong. but i do not belong and i am more like the tramp than a movie star. my skin looks white and dead in the water. i am Charlie Chaplin perhaps or maybe Woody Allen. but sarah on the other hand is lovely. she is reminiscent of Old Hollywood. she is Marilyn Monroe. and the two of us make for a pitiful juxtaposition out behind a los angeles mansion.

Right: Andrew Lane, *Untitled.* Adolescent love has its own keynotes, seen both in the photograph and the story.

"it's for the children," sarah says.

"what is?"

"the playground."

"oh," I mumble, "what does your uncle do?"

"parking lots."

for some reason "parking lots" doesn't seem to explain itself and I try again.

"what do you mean parking lots?"

sarah is unamused by my journalism.

"you know the restaurant we had lunch at yesterday, in malibu?"

"yeah."

"well, he owns that one and a lot more."

"you mean i paid three bucks valet to your uncle yesterday?"

"yep. he's the biggest parking lot company in america."

sarah floats to the other end of the pool in big black sunglasses. she's better at this pretending thing than i am. it's a big pool and i begin reading my book. the book is Women by charles bukowski. bukowski was a retired postal clerk. he said he started writing so that he could sleep until noon everyday. i am working under a similar supposition. he was also an alcoholic and maybe a nihilist, and the book consists of about a hundred or so chapters that read more like vignettes. they are short semi-pornographic accounts of the women he slept with. but maybe it's not pornography. it is realism, and besides the sex there is vivid discussion of popping pills, smoking grass, getting drunk, stealing, loathing, fighting, and death. bukowski died in 1991 and one particular passage stands out in my mind:

> "Nothing ever was in tune. People just blindly grabbed at whatever there was: communism, health foods,
> zen, surfing, ballet, hypnotism, group encounters, orgies, biking, herbs, Catholicism, weight-lifting, travel,
> withdrawal, vegetarianism, India, painting, writing. sculpting, composing, conducting, backpacking, yoga,

copulating, gambling, drinking, hanging around, frozen yogurt, Beethoven, Bach, Buddha, Christ, TM, H,
carrot juice, suicide, handmade suits, jet travel, New York City, and then it all evaporated and fell apart.
People had to find things to do while waiting to die. I guess it was nice to have a choice."

some time in the evening the sun burns out and goes down behind the brown hills. the streetlamps come on and all around the little neighborhood there is an uncomfortable silence. sarah and i are faced with the unusual reality that no one is here, that we are alone, and i begin to feel led on by charles bukowski, by a relative indifference, by sex and drugs and alcohol and existentialism.

back inside the house i push sarah against the pool table and pull her wet bikini down. her body is pink and sad and beautiful. she really is better than me.

"baby, what are you doing?"
"ssshh c'mon."
"not here."
"yeah, yeah here."
"baby . . . you're crazy. what if?"
"what if nothing? c'mon."

we do it on the table and when we finish i climb off of her exhausted. i feel a delirious light crawl through my skin and i feel bukowski's words sitting in my belly. i ask myself what a paragon of animals is man and pull a pair of trousers on.

later we drink a twelve pack of green beer and at some point we start looking for pills. i guess i should tell you that i have a thing for pills. several years ago i first found a bottle of vicodin prescribed to my father after he had back surgery. i took a couple and felt like i was a goddamned angel at a trainwreck. i began ciphering the pills until one day he caught me going through his underwear drawer in a stupor. i was sixteen years old then. we are nineteen now.

we begin in the kitchen, going through each drawer and cupboard and shelf. i find some daily vitamins. i find some triamenic. i find an eye dropper and some diarrhea medicine. but no pills.

"better look upstairs," i say, and sarah follows.

in the master bedroom we go through drawers, we look under the bed, we look in jewelry boxes. we search the closet, the bathroom, and the nightstand. the room smells of jasmine.

i can tell you that sarah's aunt wears lacy underwear. i can tell you she has an affinity for black. i can tell you that her uncle likes cowboy boots and probably has stomach trouble. but there is nothing else. they are clean. "and Goddamnit anyway."

. . .

we give up and go back downstairs. sarah cooks something in the oven and i put chopin on the radio and look around the place.

chopin calms me a bit and i find a study in the back of the house. books are a different kind of addiction for me. they are pure and beautiful. and on one of the shelves there is a Great Books collection, the kind that traveling salesmen sell in august. they look like encyclopedias: blue hardcovers, little red labels, gold names. they probably have never been read and i run my finger along the complicated names to make a selection: *The Collected Works of Plato*. i slump down in an oversized leather chair and search the table of contents. i have read *Apology*, and *Symposium*, and *Republic*. i like plato. it leads to consciousness. I decide to reed *Meno* and the print is small and difficult. it is a discussion of Virtu, a discussion of truth. i take a swig of the beer and read slowly.

the night wears on. i eat baked brie with sarah in the foyer. "Foyer." we don't have words like "foyer" back home. my father was an ironworker. my mother was a housewife. i keep the book in my lap through the evening and sarah watches Sleepless in Seattle. i can tell she is annoyed. this is not the fourth of july she had wanted. we take a shower and brush our teeth and make our way to a little yellow bedroom. it is a small room. actually it used to be a closet. the house has ten bedrooms in all. i counted them. sarah's uncle has given her the closet.

sarah is a thin girl and after the four or five beers she is drunk and falls asleep easily. but a little nightlight is on in the corner and i continue to read. it is all affecting me: the beer, bukowski, plato. earlier bukowski had felt better. but now plato does. plato feels right. during this afternoon life seemed relative. it all seemed very human. life was an encyclopedia salesman in august. i close the book to the sound of plato laughing at me.

and then suddenly i am crying. sarah is snoring. it is a pitiful juxtaposition inside a closet. i turn off the light and look out the window. perhaps this is what faulkner has described as "the conflict of the heart." there is only a sliver of moon outside, just enough moon to get under your skin, to imbue the sky with a small opaque light, and i am humiliated to know what color underwear is in the drawers upstairs. i am embarrassed at what kind of medicine is in the cabinets of this house. i feel sad and sick and dumb that i know what's under these people's bed, what's under their clothes, what kind of lives they are living, what kind of death they are having.

i grab my notebook and begin writing. it is the thirteenth notebook i have filled up since i started writing ten years ago. Yeats said that "out of the quarrel with others we make rhetoric; out of the quarrel with ourselves, poetry." i write it all down from the time i woke up this morning up through the moment of consciousness i had fifteen seconds ago.

and all around the country there are beautiful fireworks explosions in the atmosphere at the same moment that i am writing. there are hues of red and yellow and gold in the sky and it looks like colored rain. it looks like it has been sent from above.

back downstairs i have left the television on. there are some dull fireworks and the sound is muted. the house is vague and empty. i kiss sarah on the cheek and close my eyes. the moon is out of sight now and at some point i fall asleep, snoring and dreaming and getting older. and i guess it is kind of funny, Marilyn Monroe and Woody Allen asleep in a closet. my mother once found my poems under the bed and cried out loud. she asked why can't you be more like hemingway? when i told her hemingway committed suicide she just sighed and walked away. maybe it is relative.

EXTRACT FROM DAUGHTER OF FORTUNE

Isabel Allende

S HE DIDN'T KNOW WHETHER IT WAS DAY OR NIGHT, TUESDAY OR FRIDAY, whether it had been a few hours or several years since she'd met that young man. She felt that her blood had turned to froth, and she broke out in hives that faded as suddenly and inexplicably as they had appeared. She saw her beloved everywhere: in the shadows of the corners, in the shapes of the clouds, in her teacup, and most of all in her dreams . . . She needed desperately to talk with someone about her love, to analyze every detail of his brief visit, to speculate on what they should have said to each other and what they had communicated with glances, blushes, and designs, but she had no one in whom to confide . . . .She never imagined a scenario in which her love was not returned with the same depth of feeling, for to her it was impossible to believe that a love of such magnitude could have stunned only her. The mostly elementary logic and justice indicated that somewhere in the city he was suffering the same delicious torment.

Sometimes with one I love I fill myself with rage for fear I effuse unreturn'd love, but now I think there is no unreturn'd love, the pay's certain one way or another, (I loved a certain person ardently and my love was not return'd, yet out of that I have written these songs.)

—Walt Whitman

Left: Fred Astaire and Ginger Rogers embodied romance through dance with their wonderful synchronicity seeming to float on air.   **Above:** Willy Pogany in Isidora Newman's Fairy Flowers. The Lily Nymph gazes up at the sun she adores.

Left: Agnes Pelton, *Untitled.* Both painting and story enter into Other Worlds.

THE STORY OF SCAR-FACE

North American Indian Myth

SCAR-FACE WAS BRAVE BUT POOR. HIS PARENTS HAD DIED WHILE HE WAS YET A BOY, and he had no near relation. But his heart was high and he was a mighty hunter. The old man said that Scar-face had a future before him, but the young braves twitted him because of a mark across his face, left by the rending claw of a great grizzly which he had slain in close fight.

The chief of his tribe possessed a beautiful daughter, whom all the young men desired in marriage. Scar-face also had fallen in love with her, but he felt ashamed to declare his passion because of his poverty. The maiden had already repulsed half the braves of his tribe. Why, he argued, should she accept him, poor and disfigured as he was?

One day he passed her as she sat outside her lodge. He cast a penetrating glance at her—a glance which was observed by one of her unsuccessful suitors, who sneeringly remarked:

"Scar-face would marry our chief's daughter! She does not desire a man without a blemish. Ha, Scar-face, now is your chance!"

Scar-face turned upon the jeerer, and in his quiet yet dignified manner remarked that it was his intention to ask the chief's daughter to be his wife. His announcement met with ridicule, but he took no notice of it and sought the girl.

He found her by the river, pulling rushes to make baskets. Approaching, he respectfully addressed her.

"I am poor," he said, "but my heart is rich in love for you. I have no wealth of furs or pemmican. I live by my bow and spear. I love you. Will you dwell with me in my lodge and be my wife?"

The girl regarded him with bright, shy eyes peering up through lashes as the morning sun peers through the branches.

"My husband would not be poor," she faltered, "for my father, the chief, is wealthy and has abundance in his lodge. But it has been laid upon me by the Sun-god that I may not marry."

"These are heavy words," said Scar-face sadly. "May they not be recalled?"

"On one condition only," replied the girl. "Seek the Sun-god and ask him to release me from my promise. If he consents to do so, request him to remove the scar from your face as a sign that I may know that he gives me to you."

Scar-face was sad at heart, for he could not believe that the Sun-god, having chosen such a beautiful maiden for himself, would renounce her. But he gave the chief's daughter his promise that he would seek out the god in his own bright country and ask him to grant his request.

For many moons Scar-face sought the home of the Sun-god. He traversed wide plains and dense forests, crossed rivers and lofty mountains, yet never a trace of the golden gates of the golden gates of the dwelling of the God of Light could he see.

Many inquiries did he make from the wild denizens of the forest—the wolf, the bear, the badger. But none was aware of the way to the home of the Sun-god. He asked the birds, but though they flew far they were likewise in ignorance of the road thither. At last he met a wolverine who told him that he had been there himself, and promised to set him on the way. For a long and weary season they marched onward until at length they cane to a great water, too broad and too deep to cross.

As Scar-face sat despondent on the bank bemoaning his case two beautiful swans advanced from the water, and, requesting him to sit on their backs, bore him across in safety. Landing him on the other side, they showed him which way to take and left him. He had not walked far when he saw a bow and arrows lying before him. But Scar-face was punctilious and would not pick them up because they did not belong to him. Not long afterward he encountered a beautiful youth of handsome form and smiling aspect.

"I have lost a bow and arrows," he said to Scar-face. "Have you seen them?"

Scar-face told him that he had seen them a little way back, and the handsome youth praised him for his honesty in not appropriating them. He further asked him where he was bound for.

"I am seeking the Sun in his home," replied the Indian, "and I believe that I am not far from my destination."

"You are right," replied the youth. "I am the son of the Sun, Apisirahts, the Morning Star, and I will lead you to the presence of my august father."

They walked onward for a little space and then Apisirahts pointed out a great lodge, glorious with golden light and decorated with an art more curious than any that Scar-face had ever beheld. At the entrance stood a beautiful woman, the mother of Morning Star, Kokomikis, the Moon-goddess, who welcomed the footsore Indian kindly and joyously.

Then the great Sun-god appeared, wondrous in his strength and beauty as the mighty planet over which he ruled. He too greeted Scar-face kindly, and requested him to be his guest and to hunt with his son. Scar-face and the youth gladly set out for the chase. But on departing the Sun-god warned them not to venture near the Great Water, as there dwelt savage birds which might slay Morning Star.

Scar-face tarried with the Sun, his wife and child, fearful of asking his boon too speedily, and desiring to make as sure as possible of its being granted.

One day he and Morning Star hunted as usual, and the youth stole away, for he wished to slay the savage birds of which his father had spoken. But Scar-face followed, rescued the lad in imminent peril, and killed the monsters. The Sun was grateful to him for having saved his son from a terrible death, and asked him for what reason he had sought his lodge. Scar-face acquainted him with the circumstances of his love for the chief's daughter and of his quest. At once the Sun-god granted his desire.

"Return to the woman you love so much," he said, "return and make her yours. And as a sign that it is my will that she should be your wife, I make you whole."

With a motion of his bright hand the deity removed the unsightly scar. On quitting the Sun-country the god, his wife and son presented Scar-face with many good gifts, and showed him a short route by which to return to Earth-land once more.

Scar-face soon reached his home. When he sought his chief's daughter she did not know him at first, so rich was the gleaming attire he had obtained in the Sun-country. But when she at last recognized him, she fell upon his breast with a glad cry. That same day she was made his wife. The happy pair raised a 'medicine' lodge to the Sun-god, and henceforth Scar-face was called Smooth-face.

GIRLS IN THEIR SUMMER DRESSES

Irwin Shaw

FIFTH AVENUE WAS SHINING IN THE SUN WHEN THEY LEFT THE BREVOORT. THE SUN was warm, even though it was February, and everything looked like Sunday morning—the buses and the well-dressed people walking slowly in couples and the quiet buildings with the windows closed.

Michael held Frances' arm tightly as they walked toward Washington Square in the sunlight. They walked lightly, almost smiling, because they had slept late and had a good breakfast and it was Sunday. Michael unbuttoned his coat and let it flap around him in the mild wind.

Above: Alfred Stieglitz, *Dorothy True.*

"Look out," Frances said as they crossed Eighth Street. "You'll break your neck."

Michael laughed and Frances laughed with him.

"She's not so pretty," Frances said. "Anyway, not pretty enough to take a chance of breaking your neck."

Michael laughed again. "How did you know I was looking at her?"

Frances cocked her head to one side and smiled at her husband under the brim of her hat. "Mike, darling," she said.

"O.K.," he said. "Excuse me."

Frances patted his arm lightly and pulled him along a little faster toward Washington Square. "Let's not see anybody all day," she said. "Let's just hang around with each other. You and me. We're always up to the neck with people, drinking their Scotch or drinking our Scotch; we only see each other in bed. I want to go out with my husband all day long. I want him to talk only to me and listen only to me."

"What's to stop us?" Michael asked.

"The Stevensons. They want us to drop by around one o'clock and they'll drive us into the country."

"The cunning Stevensons," Mike said. "Transparent. They can whistle. They can go driving in the country by themselves."

"Is it a date?"

"It's a date."

Frances leaned over and kissed him on the tip of the ear.

"Darling," Michael said, "this is Fifth Avenue."

"Let me arrange a program," Frances said. "A planned Sunday in New York for a young couple with money to throw away."

"Go easy."

"First let's go the Metropolitan Museum of Art," Frances suggested, because Michael had said during the week he wanted to go. "I haven't been there in three years and there're at least ten pictures I want to see again. Then we can take the bus down to Radio City and watch them skate. And later we'll go down to Cavanagh's and get a steak as big as a blacksmith's apron, with a bottle of wine, and after that there's a French picture at the Film-arte that everybody says—say, are you listening to me?"

"Sure," he said. He took his eyes off the hatless girl with the dark hair, cut dancer-style like a helmet, who was walking past him.

"That's the program for the day," Frances said flatly. "Or maybe you'd just rather walk up and down Fifth Avenue."

"No," Michael said. "Not at all."

"You always look at other women," Frances said. "Everywhere. Every damned place we go."

"Now, darling," Michael said, "I look at everything. God gave me eyes and I look at women and men and subway excavations and moving pictures and the little flowers of the field. I casually inspect the universe."

"You ought to see the look in your eye," Frances said, "as you casually inspect the universe on Fifth Avenue."

"I'm a happily married man." Michael pressed her elbow tenderly. "Example for the whole twentieth century—Mr. and Mrs. Mike Loomis. Hey, let's have a drink," he said, stopping.

"We just had breakfast."

"Now listen, darling," Mike said, choosing his words with care, "It's a nice day and we both felt good and there's no reason why we have to break it up. Let's have a nice Sunday."

"All right. I don't know why I started this. Let's drop it. Let's have a good time."

They joined hands consciously and walked without talking among the baby carriages and the old Italian men in their Sunday clothes and the young women with Scotties in Washington Square Park.

"At least once a year everyone should go to the Metropolitan Museum of Art," Frances said after a while, her tone a good imitation of the tone she had used at breakfast and at the beginning of their walk "And it's nice on Sunday. There're a lot of people looking at the pictures and you get the feeling maybe Art isn't on the decline in New York City after all—"

"I want to tell you something," Michael said very seriously. "I have

Those who are faithful know only the trivial side of love: it is the faithless who know love's tragedies.

—Oscar Wilde

not touched another woman. Not once. In all the five years."

"All right," Frances said.

"You believe that, don't you?"

"All right."

They walked between the crowded benches under the scrubby city-park trees.

"I try not to notice it," Frances said, "but I feel rotten inside, in my stomach, when we pass a woman and you look at her and I see that look in your eye and that's the way you looked at me the first time. In Alice Maxwell's house. Standing there in the living room, next to the radio with a green hat on and all those people."

"I remember the hat," Michael said.

"The same look," Frances said. "And it makes me feel bad. It makes me feel terrible."

"Sh-h-h, please, darling, sh-h-h."

"I think I would like a drink now," Frances said.

They walked over to a bar on Eighth Street, not saying anything, Michael automatically helping her over curbstones and guiding her past automobiles. They sat near a window in the bar and the sun streamed in and there was a small, cheerful fire in the fireplace. A little Japanese waiter came over and put down some pretzels and smiled happily at them.

"What do you order after breakfast?" Michael asked.

"Brandy, I suppose," Frances said.

"Courvoisier," Michael told the waiter. "Two Courvoisiers."

The waiter came with the glasses and they sat drinking the brandy in the sunlight. Michael finished half his and drank a little water.

"I look at women," he said. "Correct. I don't say it's wrong or right. I look at them. If I pass them on the street, and I don't look at them, I'm fooling you, I'm fooling myself."

"You look at them as though you want them," Frances said, playing with her brandy glass. "Every one of them."

"In a way," Michael said, speaking softly and not to his wife, "in a way that's true. I don't do anything about it, but it's true."

"I know it. That's why I feel bad."

"Another brandy," Michael called. "Waiter, two more brandies."

He sighed and closed his eyes and rubbed them gently with his finger tips. "I love the way women look. One of the things I like about New York is the battalions of women. When I first came to New York from Ohio that was the first thing I noticed, the million wonderful women, all over the city. I walked around with my heart in my throat."

"A kid," Frances said. "That's a kid's feeling."

"Guess again," Michael said. "Guess again. I'm older now, I'm a man getting near middle age, putting on a little fat and I still love to walk along Fifth Avenue at three o'clock on the east side of the street between Fiftieth and Fifty-seventh Streets. They're all out then, shopping, in their furs and their crazy hats, everything all concentrated from all over the world into seven blocks—the best furs, the best clothes, the handsomest women, out to spend money and feeling good about it."

The Japanese waiter put the two drinks down, smiling with great happiness.

"Everything is all right?" he asked.

"Everything is wonderful," Michael said.

"If it's just a couple of fur coats," Frances said, "and forty-five-dollar hats."

"It's not the fur coats. Or the hats. That's just the scenery for that particular kind of woman. Understand," he said, "you don't have to listen to this."

"I want to listen."

"I like the girls in the offices. Neat, with their eyeglasses, smart, chipper, knowing what everything is about. I like the girls on Forty-fourth Street at lunchtime, the actresses, all dressed up on nothing a week. I like the salesgirls in the stores, paying attention to you first because you're a man, leaving lady customers waiting. I got all this stuff accumulated in me because I've been thinking about it for ten years and now you've asked for it and here it is."

"Go ahead," Frances said.

"When I think of New York City, I think of all the girls on parade in the city. I don't know whether it's something special with me or whether every man in the city walks around with the same feeling inside him, but I feel as though I'm at a picnic in this city. I like to sit near the women in the theaters, the famous beauties who've taken six hours to get ready and look It. And the young girls at the football games, with their red cheeks, and when the warm weather comes, the girls in their summer dresses." He finished his drink. "That's the story."

Frances finished her drink and swallowed two or three times extra. "You say you love me?"

"I love you."

"I'm pretty, too," Frances said. "As pretty as any of them."

"You're beautiful," Michael said.

"I'm good for you," Frances said, pleading. "I've made a good wife, a good housekeeper, a good friend. I'd do any damn thing for you."

"I know," Michael said. He put his hand out and grasped hers.

"You'd like to be free to—" Frances said.

"Sh-h-h."

"Tell the truth." She took her hand away from under his.

Michael flicked the edge of his glass with his finger. "O.K.," he said gently. "Sometimes I feel I would like to be free."

"Well," Frances said "any time you say."

"Don't be foolish." Michael swung his chair around to her side of the table and patted her thigh.

She began to cry silently into her handkerchief, bent over just enough so that nobody in the bar would notice. "Someday," she said, crying, "you're going to make a move."

Michael didn't say anything. He sat watching the bartender slowly peel a lemon.

"Aren't you?" Frances asked harshly. "Come on, tell me. Talk. Aren't you?"

"Maybe," Michael said. He moved his chair back again. "How the hell do I know?"

"You know," Frances persisted. "Don't you?"

"Yes," Michael said after a while, "I know."

Frances stopped crying then. Two or three snuffles into the handkerchief and she put it away and her face didn't tell anything to anybody. "At least do me one favor," she said.

"Sure."

"Stop talking about how pretty this woman is or that one. Nice eyes, nice breasts, a pretty figure, good voice." She mimicked his voice. "Keep it to yourself. I'm not interested."

Michael waved to the waiter. "I'll keep it to myself," he said.

Frances flicked the corners of her eyes. "Another brandy," she told the waiter.

"Two," Michael said.

"Yes, ma'am, yes, sir," said the waiter, backing away.

Frances regarded Michael coolly across the table. "Do you want me to call the Stevensons?" she asked. "It'll be nice in the country."

"Sure," Michael said. "Call them."

She got up from the table and walked across the room toward the telephone. Michael watched her walk, thinking what a pretty gal, what nice legs.

T O   A   C O M M O N   P R O S T I T U T E

Walt Whitman

BE COMPOSED—BE AT EASE WITH ME—I AM WALT WHITMAN, LIBERAL AND LUSTY AS NATURE,
Not till the sun excludes you do I exclude you,
Not till the waters refuse to glisten for you and the leaves to rustle for
you, do my words refuse to glisten and rustle for you.

My girl I appoint with you an appointment, and I charge you that you make
preparation to be worthy to meet me,
And I charge you that you be patient and perfect till I come.

Till then I salute you with a significant look that you do not forget me.

Right: Maxfield Parrish, *Pan by a stream,* in Scribner's Magazine, August 1910. The ancient god Pan, with his lustful nature, lives on today in every man as described in this poem by Walt Whitman.

*Variations of this song have
circulated through American culture
for nearly a hundred years.
Recorded by Elvis and filmed by
Hollywood, it is a timeless story that
exposes the shadow sides of both
women and men when they
desperately cling to bad love. This
version has been adapted by Mark
Robert Waldman.*

F R A N K I E   A N D   J O H N N I E

Traditional American Folk Ballad

Frankie and Johnnie were lovers,
O Lordie, how they could love!
They swore to be true to each other,
Just as true as the stars above.
He was her man, but he done her wrong.

Frankie, she was a good woman,
Just as everyone knows,
She gave Johnnie all of her money
But he spent it on women and clothes.
He was her man, but he done her wrong.

Johnnie went down to the tavern
And ordered a bucket of beer.
Frankie came down in an hour
Asking, "Has my Johnnie been here?
He is my man, but he's doing me wrong."

"I don't want to cause you no trouble,
I don't want to tell you no lie,
I saw that young man you call Johnnie,
With a girl named Nellie Bly.
I know he's your man, but he's doing you wrong."

Frankie went down to the hotel,
The bartender, he did not lie,
She peered through the keyhole at Johnnie,
Who was loving-up Alice Bly.
He was her man, but he was doing her wrong.

Frankie threw back her kimono.
She pulled out a pistol and shot.
Johnnie stood up and fell over,
With a bullet lodged in his heart.
He was her man, but he done her wrong.

The deputy handcuffed poor Frankie,
And took her right down to the jail.
He locked her up in a small cell,
'Cause she had no money for bail.
"He was my man, but he done me wrong."

Frankie, she turned to the sheriff:
"What do you think they will do?"
The sheriff, he said to Frankie,
"The hangman is waiting for you.
He was your man, but you done him wrong."

The judge, he says to the jury,
"The truth is as plain as you see,
Frankie, she shot up her lover,
And it's murder in the first degree.
He was her man, though he done her wrong."

Frankie went back to the jail-house,
It had no electrical fan,
She called for her little sister,
Said "Don't you marry no gamblin' man.
I had a man, but he done me wrong."

Frankie was led up the staircase,
Her life they were aiming to end,
She swore at the top of the gallows,
"There ain't no good in men,
They'll do you wrong, just as sure as you're born."

Frankie was taken to heaven
but Johnnie went straight down to hell,
There's no moral to this sad story
of two lovers who never loved well.
He was her man, but they done themselves wrong.

Above: Thomas Hart Benton, *Frankie and Johnnie.*

THE WRONG CART

Bruce Holland Rogers

HE TRAILER PARKS AND THE gated communities of any town are like circles that touch at one point, and that one point is the grocery store. Everybody's got to eat. In the rice-and-bean aisle, me and this woman got our carts mixed up. She added her wild rice blend to my cart with its ground beef, cheese spread, chips, beer, and Hungry Man dinners. I found myself pushing her cart with the kalamata olives, sun-dried tomatoes, steaks, brie, and the pork-and-beans I had just taken off the self.

Left: Andrew Lane, *Untitled.* Could we just pick up and walk off with someone else's identity?

People don't like to admit mistakes. You know how it is. Sometimes it's just easier to act like you didn't make a mistake at all, like you're doing exactly what you meant to do all along.

Her husband walked alongside the cart that had been hers, but now was mine, while she walked off towards the frozen foods aisle with my wife, who was holding our sleeping baby. Her husband thought some wine would go well with the steaks. He picked a bottle that cost three times what you could pay for a whole jug of something else, but I didn't say anything.

I could have said something while we stood in line two registers over from where my wife and this man's wife were checking out. I could have said something when we were getting into the Mercedes and our wives were getting into my rig. But the deeper you go into a mistake, the harder it is to admit it later on. Also, I was thinking about those steaks.

Before that night, I'd never been inside one of those gated communities except to pour concrete slabs for the driveways during construction. He parked the Mercedes in the garage, next to another one that was just like it, only yellow. I made a salad, salted the raw steaks, and heated up the range-top grill. In the back yard, blue light shimmered up from the swimming pool. There was a floating chair where you could sit all day if you didn't have to work.

Mail on the kitchen table was addressed to Michael and Nancy Taylor.

I served the steaks with butter. They were tender and juicy. After we finished the wine, Michael turned down the lights, massaged my shoulders, and suggested that we go to bed early. No matter how reluctant you've been to admit a mistake, there's bound to be a moment when you know that going any further will be too far.

I was about to explain about the grocery cart mix-up when I noticed the blue reflected light from the swimming pool dancing on the dining room ceiling. I remembered that floating chair. Michael was rubbing my neck, and I thought, How bad could it be?

Late the next morning, while I was sitting in that floating chair, I took a call on the cell phone. "Yeah?" I said, and this woman's voice said, "Tony? Is this Tony?"

I didn't know what to say because, yes, Tony is my name.

"Tony," the voice said, "this is Nancy. I need your help."

"Yeah," I said. "Okay." I figured we were going to have to face the music, both of us, and admit our mistake.

But she said, "I'm on break. We're pouring driveways, and Greg wants to know what's gotten into me,

I can't finish for shit. What's the secret to a good finish job?"

So I told her. Putting down a good finish to a driveway surface is one of the things I know how to do.

There were some things I did *not* know how to do. I did not know how to mix a martini the way Michael liked them. I did not know the right place to send his shirts. I did not know how to clean the pool.

Nancy and I traded phone calls. We talked about the things we needed to know, and about other things, too. She was frustrated that there wasn't really any room to move up at work. I was frustrated with sex, which was all about Michael's pleasure and not mine. She wondered how the hydrangeas were coming along. I wondered about the baby. We felt close. We had a lot in common.

Finally we met at a motel. She parked the rig on one side of the parking lot. I parked the yellow Mercedes on the other side. She registered us as Mr. and Mrs. John Smith and paid cash for the room.

Afterwards, as I drove the Mercedes home, I wondered if we weren't making a mistake. But it was too late, I told myself. Sometimes, once you start down a certain path, there just isn't any turning back.

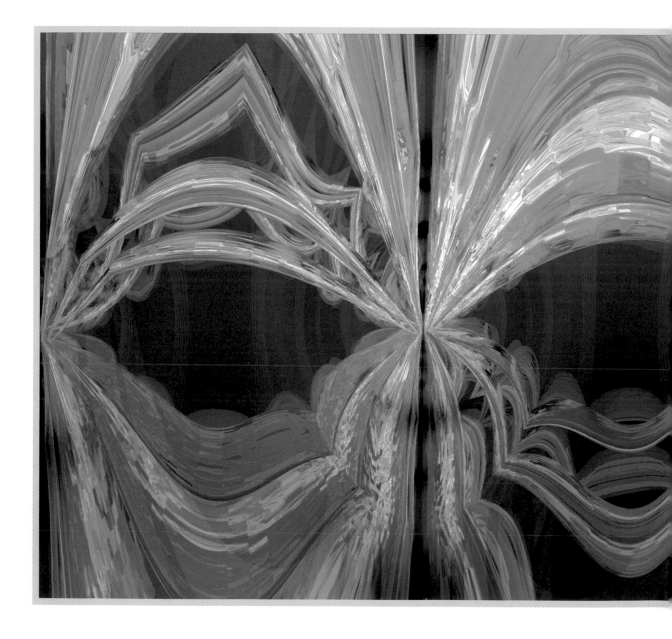

STUBBORN HUSBAND, STUBBORN WIFE

Alan B. Chinen

O NCE UPON A TIME, A HUSBAND HAD THE HABIT OF SITTING OUTSIDE HIS HOME EVERY DAY, WHILE his wife cooked their meals, swept the floor, and washed their clothes. The two quarreled constantly. "Why do you sit there doing nothing?" the wife would ask.

"I am thinking deep thoughts," the husband would reply.

"As deep as a pig's tail is long!" the wife would retort.

One morning, the calf lowed hungrily in the barn. "Go and tend the calf," the wife told her husband. "It is man's work."

"No," the man declared, "it is for men to speak and women to obey."

"Real men work!" the wife replied sharply.

"I inherited a flock of sheep from my father," the husband countered, "and a shepherd tends them and gives us wool and cheese. I provide for you, so you must feed the calf."

"Provide? Only with misery!" the woman shot back. The two argued all that morning and

Left: Cathryn Chase, *Envy*.

all that afternoon. Then, in the evening, the husband and wife both had the same idea at the same time.

"Whoever speaks first," they said simultaneously, "will feed the calf from now on!" The two nodded in agreement, and said nothing. They went to bed in silence.

The next morning, the wife awoke, lit the fire, cooked breakfast, swept the floor, and washed the clothes. Meanwhile, her husband sat on his bench, smoking his pipe. The wife knew that if she stayed home watching her husband do nothing all day, she would say something. So she put on her veil, and went to visit a friend. Her husband saw her leave, and wondered what she was up to.

A short time later, a beggar came by the house and asked the husband for food and money. The husband was about to reply, when he stopped himself. This is my wife's trick! he thought. "She is trying to make me talk." So the husband kept silent. The beggar thought the husband was a deaf-mute, and went into the house. No one was inside, but the cupboards were full of bread and cheese. So the beggar ate everything and left. The husband started to yell at the beggar, but he remembered his wager with his wife and kept silent.

A traveling barber passed by and asked the husband if he wanted his beard trimmed. The husband said nothing. This is another one of my wife's tricks! the stubborn man fumed. The barber thought he was dealing with a deaf-mute, but he wanted to he helpful, so he trimmed the husband's beard. Then the barber motioned for money. The husband did not move. The barber demanded money again, and became angry. "I will shave off your beard and cut your hair so you look like a woman!" the barber threatened. The husband refused to stir, so the barber shaved off the husband's beard, cut his hair, and left in a huff.

An old woman came up next, peddling cosmetics and secrets of

The rapid changes driven by technological advances and a changing value system have made it easy to excise human interaction—profound and trivial—from our daily lives. We are falling out of practice. We are losing our ability to do such basic things as converse and make ourselves comfortable around others. We must learn not merely to overcome this nervousness with interaction but to find solace and pleasure in the act. We must learn, too, to look more deeply at those around us in an effort to find common ground.

—Laura Pappano

beauty. Her eyesight was poor, and she mistook the husband for a young woman. "Dear lady!" the old woman exclaimed, you must not sit in public without a veil!" Especially, the old woman added to herself, when you are so ugly! The husband said nothing, so the old woman assumed he was a deaf-mute. "You poor thing," she murmured, "ugly as sin, and deaf to boot!"

The old woman had an idea, and took out her cosmetics. She put a wig on the husband's head, rouge on his cheeks, and lipstick on his mouth. "There," she declared, "you look better!" Then she motioned for payment. The husband refused to move or speak, so the old woman reached into his pocket, took all his money, and left. The husband fumed silently: I will avenge myself on my wife!

A thief then approached. He thought it odd for a young woman to be sitting outside alone. But strange situations were often profitable for him, so he went up to the woman. "Dear lady," he said, "you should not he out alone. Have you no husband or brother to look after you?"

The husband almost laughed aloud. My wife will not give up her tricks! he said to himself. The thief assumed the husband was a deaf-mute, went into the house, which was filled full of costly carpets, vases, and clothes, and packed everything in a bag. He left with his loot and waved merrily to the husband.

I will punish my wife for her tricks, the man swore to himself. By then it was midmorning, and the calf in the barn was thirsty. It broke out of its stall, and ran through the village. The wife heard the commotion, and came out from her friend's house. She caught the calf and returned home. Then she saw the strange woman sitting on her husband's bench.

"Who are you?" she demanded, "and where is my husband? I am gone only a few hours and he has taken another wife!"

"Aha!" the husband sprang up. "You spoke first, so you must tend the calf from now on!"

The wife was incredulous. "You shaved off your beard and put on rouge just to trick me!" She stormed into the house and saw that everything was gone. "What happened?" she demanded of her husband. "Who has taken all our things'?"

"The man you hired to act like a thief," the husband chortled. "But I did not fall for your deception!"

"I hired nobody!" the wife declared.

"You cannot fool me," the man boasted. "You lost the wager, and so you must tend the calf from now on."

"Foolish man!" the wife exclaimed. "You sat watching a thief steal everything from our house!"

"I knew it was only an act!" the husband gloated.

The wife could barely speak, she was so angry. "You lost your face and your fortune, and all you can think of is our wager!" She glared at her husband, and then said. "You are right, I shall tend the calf from now on. But that is because I am leaving and taking the calf with me. I will not stay with a stubborn fool like you!"

The woman walked to the village square with the calf and asked a group of children if they had seen a man go by carrying a large bag. The children pointed to the desert. In the distance they could see a man hurrying away, carrying a satchel on his back. The woman stared grimly after the thief, fastened her veil securely, picked up the calf's halter, and struck out into the desert. She caught up with the thief at an oasis. She sat across from the man, sighing and batting her eyelashes at him.

The thief was flattered by the wife's attention. "Where are you going all by yourself?" he asked her. "Have you no husband or brother to protect you?"

The wife fluttered her eyelashes at the thief and sighed. "If I did," the wife said sweetly, "would I be walking in the desert with only a calf for company?"

The two started talking and resumed their journey together. The wife kept sighing and glancing at the thief, and he soon asked her to marry him. She agreed, and so they planned to stop at the next village and have the chief marry them. By then evening had fallen, and the wife knew it was too late for a marriage ceremony. When they arrived at the village, the chief said as much, and invited them to stay with him for the night.

After everyone fell asleep, the wife arose and looked in the thief's bag. Sure enough, there were all her valuables—carpets, clothes, vases, and money! She loaded the bag on her calf and started to leave. Then she had an idea. She tiptoed into the kitchen, cooked some flour and water over a candle, and poured the dough into the thief's shoes and the shoes of the village chief. Finally she hurried into the desert with her calf.

When dawn came, the thief awoke and found his bride-to-be missing. He looked out a window and saw the woman hurrying away with his sack of loot. He rushed to put on his shoes, but found his feet would not fit in them. The dough in the shoes had hardened like a brick! The thief grabbed the shoes of the village chief, but they, they, too, were ruined. Finally, the thief ran out barefoot. The sun had risen by then, heating the desert sand, and his feet were soon blistered and burned. The thief was forced to halt.

For her part, the woman went back home, thinking about her husband. When she arrived at their house, she saw that her husband was not on his bench as usual. She ran inside and found the floor swept, the water drawn, the fire lit, and dinner cooking. But her husband was nowhere inside! She rushed into the courtyard, and there she found him, hanging laundry to dry.

"Stubborn husband," the wife exclaimed, "what are you doing?"

"I lost my face, my fortune, and my wife," the husband replied, "because I was a stubborn fool!"

The wife took the clothes from her husband, and said, "This is woman's work!" At that moment, the calf lowed, demanding water.

"I shall tend to the calf," the husband said.

"No," the wife retorted, "I shall do it." Then the two of them looked at each other and laughed. They came to an agreement, and from that day on, the husband took care of the calf and worked like any other husband, while the wife tended the house and never complained. In the evenings, when they finished their chores, they both sat down on the bench and watched the world go by.

Above: Julie Foakes, *Giles and Jess.*

M E T A M O R P H O S I S

Edwin Friedman

ONE MORNING MRS. K. AWOKE AND FOUND THAT HER HUSBAND HAD BEEN TRANSFORMED INTO A CATERPILLAR. HE was moving about slowly in the corner of the room usually reserved for the floor lamp, which had been sent out to be fixed.

Understanding immediately that this would necessitate changes in their marriage, Mrs. K. walked softly over to where the insect was standing and, trying carefully not to frighten him, reached over and began to caress his fur.

As soon as Mrs. K. touched him, however, the caterpillar curled up and refused to move. Surprised by the response, Mrs. K. tried to stroke her husband more gently and then, very slowly, tried to uncurl him, but he stiffened.

"There, there," she said. "I'm not going to hurt you. Don't be afraid." The caterpillar was unmoved. Mrs. K. tried again. "I still care," she said. "We can still be close," she continued, whereupon she cupped the palm of her hand so as to provide a snug, cradle-like saucer. This would enable her husband to feel safe yet at the same time also allow him to straighten out. She let her hand roll a little to see if she could jar him into moving, but the caterpillar's response was totally passive. He simply let himself slide with the motion of her hand. At one point the caterpillar almost slipped over the edge of her fingers—he was still curled in a fur like ball—so that Mrs. K. had to bring her other hand up quickly to make sure her husband didn't fall.

After this fright, however, her mood began to change. "Please," Mrs. K. implored. "Try to understand our situation. This is not going to be easy at all. I'm trying my best. The least I could expect from you is some acceptance." Still she felt no response. In fact, he seemed even more rigid than before.

She placed him down on the floor and continued to talk. "Perhaps," she thought, "if I did not hold on so tight he would show some sign of life." But the caterpillar remained still. "Would you like something to eat?" she asked, never asking herself what she would bring him. "You know, I'm going to have to go out pretty soon,

and I'm somewhat afraid to leave you here all alone." Her husband remained impassive.

"Perhaps it's too cold in here," she thought, and, taking her husband in her hand again, Mrs. K. walked over to the window left ajar for the morning air and closed it tight. "There, you see, now it will be more pleasant."

She returned to the corner where she had first found him and tore a large leaf from a plant near the couch, placed it neatly on the floor, and gingerly put her husband down on the leaf to see if a more natural habitat would stimulate a response. But still the caterpillar did not budge. Her mood changed again.

Above: Julie Foakes, *Untitled.*

"You know," said Mrs. K. a little testily, "I think I've been willing to adapt more than most women, but you can't expect me to go on like this if you are not going to be more cooperative." Nothing. "I'm not even asking you to speak. Good God, I don't even know if you can anymore! And I'm not saying you have to. But I need to have some idea of what you want. I mean, you can't leave this all up to me. Would you prefer to be in a box?" And so Mrs. K. continued talking to her husband until she began to wonder if she was only talking to herself.

Again she picked up her husband. He seemed to be even stiffer. Suddenly she put him right in front of her, at eye level, and squeezed. Nothing. Resisting, somehow, the urge to squeeze harder, she reached down and with a small stick began to poke the caterpillar. First she just touched him lightly to see if he would stir. Nothing. She prodded him harder. The caterpillar allowed himself to be rolled over by the poke. Then Mrs. K. began systematically to probe. Perhaps there was a soft spot, an area that was more vulnerable, and she began to examine her husband's furrows lengthwise along his body, taking care not to touch the head. Then she probed perpendicularly along the dark contoured circles. Neither the position of the poke nor the degree of force elicited a response. The caterpillar reeled or rolled back according to how Mrs. K. pushed. Not a single movement of the caterpillar could with certainty have ascribed to his own will. Finally, fearful that she might hurt him, Mrs. K. dropped the stick.

Her husband was now curled so tight that no light could be seen coming through the coil. The thought ran through Mrs. K. that she had killed him. How would she know? There was no blood. Would he get cold if he was dead? She picked up the stick again and poked one more time. Still, nothing.

Mrs. K. tried to assess her situation. It was clear that she must now take responsibility for everything, though that would not be too different from before. She would, of course, do all the work around the house, and unless it turned out that her husband could, in fact, talk, she would continue to take all initiative in their relationship. Camaraderie, not that there had been that much in the past, was clearly out of the question. On the other hand, if he would at least be willing to move a little on his own, that would certainly help.

Mrs. K. went into her closet, where she found a large shoebox. She took the top and folded back its edges so that it could serve as a ramp, went outside and gathered grass and leaves, placed a few aphids under a stick, and brought everything back to the corner of her bedroom that was to become her husband's place. She set the box down, put the ramp into position, and tried to show her husband how he could use the cover to get into the box. "Look, honey," she said soothingly. "I've made you a place where you can be secure. I'll try to change the leaves every day, and, while I don't know yet what you eat, I'll try to find out. The library must have a book on caterpillars." She picked her husband up again and, anticipating that he would begin to crawl along her arm, placed him on her lap. Nothing. The caterpillar just lay there on its side, curled in an oval, asleep or maybe dead.

Over the next several weeks Mrs. K. learned to adapt to the change. She continued to care for her husband, although he showed no response. The only way she knew he wasn't dead was that whenever she left the room for long periods of time, the caterpillar, upon her return, would always be in a different part of his box. However, in her presence he never moved.

Noticing this fact, Mrs. K. often pretended to go away, but, once having left the room, she would peer back from behind the door, hiding herself carefully so that the caterpillar could not sense her presence. Sometimes she would stay this way for hours. But he never showed any signs of life. Yet, at other times, she could be away for only minutes, and by the time she returned, the caterpillar had made his way completely to the other side of its box.

Eventually, whether through boredom or fatigue, Mrs. K. found herself thinking less and less about her husband. This bothered her in some ways, yet the freedom it engendered enabled her to return to thinking about herself. Then she received an invitation from an old friend to visit for a while. At first she said no. How could she leave her husband alone for so long? But at her friend's urging, she finally accepted, and after taking great care to put the box in a protected place, high on a closet shelf, filled with grass for comfort and for food, she left her husband alone for the first time in years.

During that visit, she completely stopped thinking about him. In fact, when she finally returned home, it was several days before she remembered the box. Quickly she rushed to the closet and anxiously looked in. The caterpillar was gone.

Had he been eaten? Could he have gone away? She was remonstrating with herself about her failure be more concerned when the front door suddenly opened. There he stood, her husband, in the flesh. Mrs. K. could not believe her eyes. He rushed over to her, kissed her passionately, embracing Mrs. K. with a firm affection she had not experienced since their earliest days together.

"My God," he said, "where have you been? I thought I'd lost you."

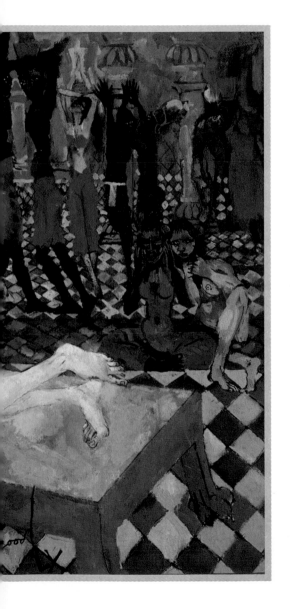

WOODWORKER

Nancy Kilpatrick

AILEEN HAMMERED IN THE FINAL NAIL. SHE RAISED AN ARM and used her rolled shirt sleeve to blot sweat from her forehead as she stepped back for a critical look.

The grain was straight, the lid level, dovetails snugly joined. Tomorrow night she would use coarse sandpaper, followed by a session with medium paper, then fine. She thought about using the sander Larry had bought her last Christmas but, God, she'd always hated machines, and the power supply here wasn't very good. And more important, the particles pressing the back of the paper as they rode the wood felt sensuous. Got that from her Nana, who had preferred old-style woodworking. Tradition, certainly; a bit late to think about changing her ways.

Left: Philip Evergood, *Ancient Queen.* The archetype of the devouring woman is often associated with a female that is hag-like and ancient, but powerful and controlling, as in this painting. In the story, the concept is taken a stage further.

Aileen swept the floor of shavings. She used a ragged t-shirt to wipe clean the steel-edged plane, then the file and rasp, and hung each in its spot on the wall. Nana had bequeathed her these tools, just as she had passed down the love of working with fine woods by hand. A love that connected the female line.

Finally Aileen picked up the sharp half-inch chisel and honed the beveled edge against a whetstone. The birch handle had worn in one spot, where the thumbs of generations of women had gripped it. Nana had been given the chisel by her grandmother when she reached puberty. With it, she had also been handed two branches and no-nonsense instructions on slicing the end of one into a mortise and the end of the other branch into a corresponding tenon. She said it had taken the better part of a week to fit the parts together just so before she presented the joint to *her* grandmother. "She barely glanced at it and, lickety-split, handed me two new branches." The process was repeated over eighteen months. One joint a week at first, then two, then three until finally, one a day. Her Nana, frustrated, had almost given up but, somehow, she'd stuck it out. "By the end I was darned good with a chisel," Aileen recalled her saying, "and I could sure make the parts fit right."

Nana had taught her in the same way, so Aileen understood the frustration. She also knew how to join two halves perfectly so that for all intents and purposes they became inseparable.

One last look at her handiwork and reluctantly she headed up the dark stairs into a wall of heat, squinting at the light in the kitchen above.

"What's for dinner?" Larry, drying dishes at the kitchen counter, wanted to know. He snaked an arm around her waist as she tried to pass. Fingers found her left nipple through the soft fabric. Hot lips pressed against her sweaty neck. The heat made her cranky and the last thing she wanted was love.

"Meatloaf." She pulled away. "And scalloped potatoes, if you peel them for me. Otherwise fries."

"Fries'll do." He sat at the table and stretched out his denim-covered legs across the narrow room, forcing her to step over them to get to the refrigerator. It was more foreplay and she was in no mood for it.

She opened the top of the refrigerator, aware of how his gaze stroked her from across the room. The freezer light was dead. White mist from the frosty darkness wafted out and she fantasized about living alone in an igloo, in a place that was all ice and snow like the Arctic, where some of the year you'd be blessed with twenty-four hours of cool darkness. You wouldn't have to swelter under just a fan. Or fear heat stroke. You wouldn't have to worry about scorching sunlight burning you to a crisp. You could live your natural life in peace.

As usual, lately, Aileen wasn't hungry. For the last six months, since they'd been in this oppressive climate, she felt as though she'd been steadily shrinking, as if the heat had been shriveling her. While Larry ate, she pushed nearly burnt potato sticks around her dinner plate and stared out the window at the pallid moon imprisoned by the muggy night sky. She hadn't wanted to move to Manila, where the weather made the days impossible and the nights nearly so. But Larry's job forced him to do field research. Forced them to leave North America and all that was familiar and be in this strange part of the world.

Outside, rubber trees with stunned leaves hung paralyzed in the dense air. Still. Waiting. Deciding whether to live or die in the sultry climate.

The next evening, when the scalding sun had set, Aileen headed down to the basement, and they were lucky to have a basement—most of the houses here didn't. Brick walls and an earth floor kept the room degrees cooler than the rest of the house. It made a difference and she preferred being here. If it weren't for Larry, she would be in the basement both night and day. She could work here, and that kept her sane.

She stretched out the sanding for an hour and a half, intoxicated by the sweet, woodscented air. She mixed sawdust and white bond glue together and filled in accidental gouges. Then she mixed the stain.

Just like Nana, Aileen hated to stain a pale wood. Still, if she could blend the pigments right, the swirling grain would be accented rather than overwhelmed. Exotic hardwoods were her favorites, one of the few benefits of living in Southeast Asia. The compressed fibers flowed like sinewy muscles, the pores received like human skin. She ran a hand slowly over the smooth surface and felt a quiver run through her body, as if she were caressing a lover. The living wood was solid, hard to damage, enduring in this hostile climate.

As Aileen rubbed in the pungent oil stain, a drop of sweat dripped off the tip of her nose and landed on the wood, sinking into and melding with it. She thought about the heat and how it was getting worse. The last month had been bad. She'd stayed in bed during the day, when Larry was home, then would sneak down to the basement the minute he left. And she was up most of the night while he slept. It seemed a bit easier to breathe at night. Hiding in the basement. Hiding from Larry. And this landscape, so unlike what she was accustomed to that it felt alien.

Of course he'd noticed. She felt him studying her all the time, the way he examined the local insects. Watching. Waiting. Like some predator ready to pounce on a weaker species. But she'd managed to avoid him, for the most part. It meant sleeping upstairs in the heat of the day when she'd have rather been enveloped by the cooler basement air. A necessary sacrifice. But it wasn't his way to ask a lot of questions nor hers to answer very many.

Last week he'd come halfway down the basement just before sunrise, when she was still cutting the rough lumber, and stood on the steps. Waiting. "Aren't you coming to bed?" he finally said in a needy voice. When she didn't respond, he stomped upstairs and slammed the door. She knew he didn't feel any more comfortable in the cool dark than she felt in the hot light. They had their differences, and this was a big one.

Her eye scanned the wet wood. The stain would dry overnight. By tomorrow she'd have to decide whether to varnish or shellac. Chemicals preserved better over time and repelled moisture too, but she preferred the natural look of shellac. Her Nana had favored shellac, too, and she'd told Aileen all about the lac scale, an insect in this part of the world, one of the ones Larry studied. How the female excretes resin onto the twig of a fake banyan tree, creating a safe place in which to live. And die. "Its her home," Nana had said, "like a turtle's shell is home to a turtle." Larry's books had told her more. The sticky glue-like resin protected the lac scale from predators and other dangers in the environment, attracted potential mates, and snared meals. That resin formed the basis of shellac.

The idea appealed to her: a natural substance produced by a creature dwelling in a tree, applied to an object made from a tree trunk. Ultimately the wood would rot and form the new earth in which a new tree might grow. It was a cycle made familiar to her by her Nana: birth, death, rebirth.

T he fireball sun seared her flesh and blinded her with its yellow glare. The heat weighed against her body; she felt heavy and clumsy. Sluggish. When it set, she stumbled down to the basement, muscles flaccid, the lining of her brain inflamed.

Where love rules, there is no will to power; and where power predominates, there love is lacking. The one is the shadow of the other.

—Carl Gustav Jung

Right: Andrew Lane, *Untitled.*

Aileen breathed shallowly. Each brush stroke of shellac was a torturous labor. Still, she felt vindicated that she had chosen this forgiving substance. Varnish would have required precision she could not muster. Even before the first coat of shellac dried, she began applying the next. Layer upon gummy layer blended together with no differentiation. No division. It was nearly dry in an hour, about the time the floorboards above her head squeaked.

Larry stood at the top of the cellar stairs peering into the dark basement. He watched Aileen, brush in hand, step into the shaft of light filtering down from the kitchen. Her skin was so fair. So unprotected. Unlike him, he knew she had a hard time with the heat and humidity.

He was seriously worried about her. Down here every night. Alone. They were never together anymore, since they'd moved here. When had they last had sex? It wasn't healthy.

Beside her left hip, the light from above illuminated a triangular wedge of shiny wood. The hairs on the back of his neck rose. What in hell was she building, anyway? Light from the kitchen caught the liquid in Aileen's eyes. For a split second an optical illusion made her eyes appear entirely white. Her bent arm held up the brush like a flag of surrender; he noticed her fragile-looking wrist bone jutting out. Funny how that bone had always turned him on. That and the way her collarbone protruded, delicately exposed where her shirt collar lay open.

Her skin was sweat-slicked. Even through the shellac, he could smell her from here.

"Come up to bed," he coaxed.

Aileen lay the brush down, started slowly up the steps, stopped. She glanced up at him through dark lashes and breathed, "Come down."

Larry hated dark basements. Had since he was a child. Dank air. Gritty earth that clotted his nostrils with the odor of eons of decay. The atmosphere reminded him of cemeteries. The basement itself felt like a grave.

Her lips twisted into a smile. She backed down the stairs, unbuttoning her blouse. The shadows swallowed her.

"Aileen?" he called.

Wood scraped against wood. The small segment of wood lit by the kitchen light swayed like a tree branch. Unnerved, Larry gripped the railing and took a step down. The air cooled. "Honey? Come on up."

A sound of shuffling. Wood creaking. Aileen's short dark hair flashed through the lighted triangle as she lay back. Within that yellow illumination, like an artistic photograph framed in darkness, one side of her fragile collar bone pressed suggestively against her skin. A round slick breast, the nipple a glistening eye gazing directly into his, mesmerized him. That little section of flesh rose and fell and quivered as she breathed. The scent from her body mingled with the potent resin to create a sweet musky perfume.

"Close the door," she whispered.

Larry did. Surrounded by darkness, he felt his way down, her earthy scent guiding him.

He reached out, low, and touched cool tacky wood. His fingers crawled up and over the edge to find her. Sticky firm flesh yielded to the pressure of his touch. He wondered what made her sweat so thick.

Aileen pulled him down on top of her. The exotic wood creaked under the double weight but held them. She ripped his shirt away while he worked on his pants. He crawled further up her body, shivering, fear or cold or passion, she could not tell which. There was only a vague predatory instinct emanating from him that she could sense; she felt safe enough.

Her chisel-sharp teeth clamped onto his broad shoulder, piercing clammy skin. He howled and squirmed, but her sticky sweat bonded their flesh and, in truth, he did not really resist. And when they joined, it was perfect, as perfect as Aileen always knew it would be. As her Nana had told her it could be.

Cool pale wood beneath her. The familiar aroma of shellac seeping into her pores. She and Larry encased in this sheltered environment. Now that she had finally adapted, she could stay here the rest of her natural life. In complete comfort and safety. Mating. Eating. Producing the next woodworker.

EXCERPT FROM THE OVAL PORTRAIT

Edgar Allan Poe

SHE WAS A MAIDEN OF RAREST BEAUTY, AND NOT MORE LOVELY THAN FULL OF GLEE. AND EVIL WAS THE HOUR WHEN she saw, and loved, and wedded the painter. He, passionate, studious, austere, and having already a bride in his Art: she a maiden of rarest beauty, and not more lovely than full of glee; all light and smiles, and frolicsome as the young fawn; loving and cherishing all things; hating only the Art which was her rival; dreading only the pallet and brushes and other untoward instruments which deprived her of the countenance of her lover. It was thus a terrible thing for this lady to hear the painter speak of his desire to portray even his young bride. But she was humble and obedient, and sat meekly for many weeks in the dark high turret-chamber where the light dripped upon the pale canvas only from overhead. But he, the painter, took glory in his work, which went on from hour to hour, and from day to day. And he was a passionate, and wild, and moody man who became lost in reveries; so that he *would* not see that the light which fell so ghastly in that lone turret withered the health and the spirits of his bride, who pined visibly to all but him. Yet she smiled on and still on, uncomplainingly, because she saw that the painter (who had high renown) took a fervid and burning pleasure in his task, and wrought day and night to depict her who so loved him, yet who grew daily more dispirited and weak. And in sooth some one who beheld the portrait spoke of its resemblance in low words, as of a might marvel, and a proof not less of the power of the painter than of his deep love for her whom he depicted so surpassingly well. But at length, as the labor drew nearer to its conclusion, there were admitted none into the turret; for the painter had grown wild with the ardor of his work, and turned his eyes from the canvas rarely, even to regard the countenance of his wife. And he *would* not see that the tints which he spread upon the canvas were drawn from the cheeks of her who sat beside him. And when many weeks had passed, and but little remained to do, save one brush upon the mouth and one tint upon the eye, the spirit of the lady again flickered up as the flame within the socket of the lamp. And then the brush was given, and then the tint was placed; and, for one moment, the painter stood entranced before the work which he had wrought; but in the next, while he yet gazed, he grew tremulous and very pallid, and aghast, and crying with a loud voice, "This is indeed *Life* itself!" turned suddenly to regard his beloved: *She was dead!*

Left: Marilyn Monroe adjusts her make-up, next to a movie camera and in a crowd of people, 1956. Marilyn's life is in itself a legend and echoes the story's theme of the power of art to destroy what it portrays. In both cases, love or the need for love leaves the subject vulnerable to this exploitation.

SONG OF THE PASSIONATE LOVER

From the *Yokut*

Mary Austin

COME *NOT NEAR MY SONGS,*
You who are not my lover,
Lest from that ambush
Leaps my heart upon you!

When my songs are glowing
As an almond thicket
With the bloom upon it,
Lies my heart in ambush
All amid my singing;
Come not near my songs,
You who are not my lover!

Do not hear my songs,
You who are not my lover!
Over-sweet the heart is
Where my love has bruised it,
Breathe you not that fragrance,
You who are not my lover,
Do not stoop above my heart
With its languor on you,
Lest I should not know you,
From my own, belovèèd,
Lest from out my singing
Leaps my heart upon you!

Right: Georgia O'Keeffe, *Red Hills with Flowers.*

Sarah & Tony Pletts, Wedding Shrine. This shrine was created especially for the wedding ceremony as a celebration of the couple's lives, both individually and together. No-one anticipates that the optimism of the wedding day will turn into the kind of relationship in this story.

MR. PREBLE GETS RID OF HIS WIFE

James Thurber

Mr. Preble was a plump middle-aged lawyer in Scarsdale. He used to kid with his stenographer about running away with him. "Let's run away together," he would say, during a pause in dictation. "All righty," she would say.

One rainy Monday afternoon, Mr. Preble was more serious about it than usual.

"Let's run away together," said Mr. Preble.

"All righty," said his stenographer. Mr. Preble jingled the keys in his pocket and looked out the window.

"My wife would be glad to get rid of me," he said.

"Would she give you a divorce?" asked the stenographer.

"I don't suppose so," he said. The stenographer laughed.

"You'd have to get rid of your wife," she said.

Mr. Preble was unusually silent at dinner that night. About half an hour after coffee, he spoke without looking up from his paper.

"Let's go down in the cellar," Mr. Preble said to his wife.

"What for?" she said, not looking up from her book.

"Oh, I don't know," he said. "We never go down in the cellar any more. The way we used to."

"We never did go down in the cellar that I remember," said Mrs. Preble. "I could rest easy the balance of my life if never went down in the cellar." Mr. Preble was silent for several minutes.

"Supposing I said it meant a whole lot to me" began Mr. Preble.

"What's come over you?" his wife demanded. "It's cold down there and there is absolutely nothing to do."

"We could pick up pieces of coal," said Mr. Preble. "I might get up some kind of a game with pieces of coal."

"I don't want to," said his wife. "'Anyway, I'm reading."

"Listen," said Mr. Preble, rising and walking up and down. "Why won't you come down in the cellar? You could read down there, as far as that goes."

"There isn't a good enough light down there," she said, "and anyway, I'm not going to go down in the cellar. You may as well make up your mind to that."

"Gee whiz!" said Mr. Preble, kicking at the edge of a rug. "Other people's wives go down in the cellar. Why is it you never want to do anything? I come home-worn out from the office and you won't even go down in the cellar with me. God knows it isn't very far—it isn't as if I was asking you to go to the movies or some place."

"I don't want to *go!*" shouted Mrs. Preble. Mr. Preble sat down on the edge of a davenport.

"All right, all *right,*" he said. He picked up the newspaper again. "I wish you'd let me tell you more about it. It's—kind of a surprise."

"Will you quit harping on that subject?" asked Mrs. Preble.

"Listen," said Mr. Preble, leaping to his feet. "I might as well tell you the truth instead of beating around the bush. I want to get rid of you so I can marry my stenographer. Is there anything especially wrong about that? People do it every day. Love is something you can't control—"

"We've been all over that," said Mrs. Preble. "I'm not going to go all over that again."

"I just wanted you to know how things are," said Mr. Preble. "But you have to take everything so literally. Good Lord, do you suppose I really wanted to go down there and make up some silly game with pieces of coal?"

"I never believed that for a minute," said Mrs. Preble. "I knew all along you wanted to get me down there and bury me."

"You can say that now—after I told you," said Mr. Preble. "But it would never have occurred to you if I hadn't."

"You didn't tell me; I got it out of you," said Mrs. Preble. "Anyway, I'm always two steps ahead of what you're thinking."

"You're never within a mile of what I'm thinking," said Mr. Preble.

"Is that so? I knew you wanted to bury me the minute I set foot in this house tonight." Mrs. Preble held him with a glare.

"Now that's just plain damn exaggeration," said Mr. Preble, considerably annoyed. "You knew nothing of the sort. As a matter of fact, I never thought of it till just a few minutes ago."

"It was in the back of your mind," said Mrs. Preble. "I suppose this filing woman put you up to it."

"You needn't get sarcastic," said Mr. Preble. "I have plenty of people to file without having her file. She doesn't know anything about this. She isn't in on it. I was going to tell her you had gone to visit some friends and fell over a cliff. She wants me to get a divorce."

"That's a laugh," said Mrs. Preble. "*That's* a laugh. You may bury me, but you'll never get a divorce."

"She knows that! I told her that," said Mr. Preble. "I mean—I told I'd never get a divorce."

"Oh, you probably told her about burying me, too," said Mrs. Preble.

"That's not true," said Mr. Preble, with dignity. "That's between you and me. I was never going to tell a soul."

"You'd blab it to the whole world; don't tell me," add Mrs. Preble. "I know you." Mr. Preble puffed at his cigar.

"I wish you were buried now and it was all over with," he said.

"Don't you suppose you would get caught, you crazy thing?" she said. "They always get caught. Why don't you go to bed? You're just getting yourself worked up over nothing."

"I'm not going to bed," said Mr. Preble. "I'm going to bury you in the cellar. I've got my mind made up to it. I don't know how I could make it any plainer."

"Listen," cried Mrs. Preble, throwing her book down, "will you be satisfied and shut up if I go down in the cellar? Can I have a little peace if I go down in the cellar? Will you let me alone then?"

"Yes," said Mr. Preble. "But you spoil it by taking that attitude."

"Sure, sure, I always spoil everything. I stop reading right in the middle of a chapter. I'll never know how the story comes out—but that's nothing to you."

"Did I make you start reading the book?' asked Mr. Preble. He opened the cellar door. "Here, you go first."

"Brrr," said Mrs. Preble, starting down the steps. "It's *cold* down here! You *would* think of this, at this time of year! Any other husband would have buried his wife in the summer."

"You can't arrange these things just whenever you want to," said Mr. Preble. "I didn't fall in love with this girl till late fall."

"Anybody else would have fallen in love with her long before that. She's been around for years. Why is it you always let other men get in ahead of you? Mercy, but it's dirty down here! What have you got there?"

"I was going to hit you over the head with this shovel," said Mr. Preble.

"You were, huh?' said Mrs. Preble. "Well, get that out of your mind. Do you want to leave a great big clue right here in the middle of everything where the first detective that comes snooping around will find it? Go out in the street and find some piece of iron or something—something that doesn't belong to you."

"Oh, all right," said Mr. Preble. "But there won't be any piece of iron in the street. Women always expect men to pick up a piece of iron anywhere."

"If you look in the right place you'll find it," said Mrs. Preble. "And don't be gone long. Don't you dare stop in at the cigar store. I'm not going to stand down here in this cold cellar all night and freeze."

"All right," said Mr. Preble. "I'll hurry."

"And shut that *door* behind you!" she screamed after him. "Where were you born—in a barn?"

Right: Jacob Lawrence, *The Wedding.*

Left: Sarah Pletts, *Entwined figures*. A couple's lives may become inextricably entwined, even beyond the breakdown of the marriage.   **Right:** Philip Guston, *Couple in Bed*.

THE SOCK

Lydia Davis

MY HUSBAND IS MARRIED TO A DIFFERENT WOMAN NOW, SHORTER THAN I AM, ABOUT FIVE FEET TALL, SOLIDLY BUILT, and of course he looks taller than he used to and narrower, and his head looks smaller. Next to her I feel bony and awkward and she is too short for me to look her in the eye, though I try to stand or sit at the right angle to do that. I once had a clear idea of the sort of woman he should marry when he married again, but none of his girlfriends was quite what I had in mind and this one least of all.

They came out here last summer for a few weeks to see my son, who is his and mine. There were some touchy moments, but there were also some good times, though of course even the good times were a little uneasy. The two of them seemed to expect a lot of accommodation from me, maybe because she was sick—she was in pain and sulky, with circles under her eyes. They used my phone and other things in my house. They would walk up slowly from the beach to my house and shower there, and later walk away clean in the evening with my son between them, hand in hand. I gave a party, and they came and danced with each other, impressed my friends and stayed till the end. I went out of my way for them, mostly because of our boy. I thought we should all get along for his sake. By the end of their visit I was tired.

The night before they went, we had a plan to eat out in a Vietnamese restaurant with his mother. His mother was flying in from another city, and then the three of them were going off together the next day, to the Midwest. His wife's parents were giving them a big wedding party so that all the people she had grown up with, the stout farmers and their families, could meet him.

When I went into the city that night to where they were staying, I took what they had left in my house that I had found so far: a book, next to the closet door, and somewhere else a sock of his. I drove up to the building, and I saw my husband out on the sidewalk flagging me down. He wanted to talk to me before I went inside. He told me his mother was in bad shape and couldn't stay with them, and he asked me if I would please take her home with me later. Without thinking I said I would. I was forgetting the way she would look at the inside of my house and how I would clean the worst of it while she watched.

In the lobby, they were sitting across from each other in two armchairs, these two small women, both beautiful in different ways, both wearing lipstick, different shades, both frail, I thought later, in different ways. The reason they were sitting here was that his mother was afraid to go upstairs. It didn't bother her to fly in an airplane, but she couldn't go up more than one story in an apartment building. It was worse now than it had been. In the old days she could be on the eighth floor if she had to, as long as the windows were tightly shut.

Before we went out to dinner my husband took the book up to the apartment, but he had stuck the sock in his back pocket without thinking when I gave it to him out on the street and it stayed there during the meal in the restaurant, where his mother sat in her black clothes at the end of the table opposite an empty chair, sometimes playing with my son, with his cars, and sometimes asking my husband and then me and then his wife questions

We are never so defenseless against suffering as when we love, never so forlornly unhappy as when we have lost our love object or its love.

—Sigmund Freud

about the peppercorns and other strong spices that might be in her food. Then after we all left the restaurant and were standing in the parking lot he pulled the sock out of his pocket and looked at it, wondering how it had got there.

It was a small thing, but later I couldn't forget the sock, because here was this one sock in his back pocket in a strange neighborhood way out in the eastern part of the city in a Vietnamese ghetto, by the massage parlors, and none of us really knew this city but we were all here together and it was odd, because I still felt as though he and I were partners, we had been partners a long time, and I couldn't help thinking of all the other socks of his I had picked up, stiff with his sweat and threadbare on the sole, in all our life together from place to place, and then of his feet in those socks, how the skin shone through at the ball of the foot and the heel where the weave was worn down; how he would lie reading on his back on the bed with his feet crossed at the ankles so that his toes pointed at different corners of the room; how he would then turn on his side with his feet together like two halves of a fruit; how, still reading, he would reach down and pull off his socks and drop them in little balls on the floor and reach down again and pick at his toes while he read; sometimes he shared with me what he was reading and thinking, and sometimes he didn't know whether I was there in the room or somewhere else.

I couldn't forget it later, even though after they were gone I found a few other things they had left, or rather his wife had left them in the pocket of a jacket of mine—a red comb, a red lipstick, and a bottle of pills. For a while these things sat around in a little group of three on one counter of the kitchen and then another, while I thought I'd send them to her, because I thought maybe the medicine was important, but I kept forgetting to ask, until finally I put them away in a drawer to give her when they came out again, because by then it wasn't going to be long, and it made me tired all over again just to think of it.

TO WOMEN WHO SLEEP ALONE

Amy Uyematsu

MY MOTHER DOESN'T UNDERSTAND A WORLD WITH NO MAN IN IT
tells me I waste too much time
forgets I used to spend hours playing by myself.

I don't tell her what sleeping alone is really like
the sweet oils no one but me can rub into my skin.
I look at my body again
no longer as pretty
all the young men I've sent away
will not be coming back.

lately my body's scent fills every room to smother me
I wonder if any man can still enjoy its taste
a darker odor.
every month my blood flows harder
an ache building within my thighs
a real part of me dying—
I want to let in the smell of trees and wind after it's rained.

there's a small grey bird outside my house
who keeps building
her nest with pine needles.
every evening the wind scatters her work
but she returns the next day with new twigs
determined to make a home here.

I'm not one of those women
who can make up their minds
just like that
to find a man again—
something my mother never taught me.

Left: Georgia O'Keeffe, *White Shell with Red.*

THE BOY

Joyce Carol Oates

THERE WAS THIS BOY NAMED KIT, ALL SEMESTER HE PESTERED ME WITH LOVE, CALLED OUT HEY GOOD-LOOKING ON the street, after class he'd hang around eyeing me, Hey teach you're a peach, smart aleck giggly staring, wet brown eyes, smooth downy skin, didn't look fourteen but he said he was seventeen which might have been true. I said, All right damn you, I drove us out to this place I knew in the woods, a motel meant to be a lodge, fake logs with fake knotholes, I brought a six-pack of beer along, the room smelled of damp and old bedclothes, somebody's deodorant or maybe Air-Wick, bedspread that hadn't been changed in a long time. It's my strategy to praise, actually I mean everything I say, God I wanted him to feel good, there was a lot of fooling around, getting high, quick wisecracks you roar your head off at but can't remember five minutes later, we were both getting excited, Hey let's dance, we got high and fell across the bed tangling and tickling. I opened his pants and took hold of him but he was soft, breathing fast and shallow, was he afraid? but why? of *me*? hey why? I blew in his ear and got him giggling, I teased and said, Okay kid now's your chance, Mommy ain't anywhere near, kissed and tickled and rubbed against him, God I was hot, down the hall somebody played a radio loud and then a door slammed and you couldn't hear it, now I was flying high and spinning going fast around a turn in the mountains, Oooooo, hair streaming out behind me like it hasn't done in fifteen years, I was crying no I was laughing, wanted to get him hard damn it, big and inside me like a man, then I'd tell him how great he was, how fantastic, it would make me happy too, not strung out, part-time shitty teaching jobs that I had to drive twenty-three miles one way to get to, thirty miles the other, and pouches under my eyes and a twisty look that scares the nice shy kids. But he never did get hard, it felt like something little that's been skinned, naked and velvety like a baby rabbit, he was squirming like I'd hurt him or he was afraid I might hurt him, finally he said, I guess I don't love you, I guess I want to go home, but I didn't even hear it, I was thinking Oh fuck it the beer's going to be warm, I closed my eyes seeing the road tilt and spin and something about the sky, filmy little clouds that knock your heart out they're so beautiful, Hey let's dance, kid, I said giggling, let's knock the shit out of this room, he was laughing, maybe he was crying and his nose was running, I just lay there thinking, All right, kid, all right you bastards, this is it.

Right: Sarah Pletts, *Stephen at the basin.*

"*The Light of His Life*"

THE CIGAR

Robert Fulghum

YOU MIGHT AS WELL KNOW NOW. A CIGAR IS THE CENTERPIECE of what follows. And you might as well also know that I have been known to smoke one of those things from time to time, despite what I know about all the good reasons not to. I'm just assuming that you sometimes do something of your own that you shouldn't do, either, and will understand. Moreover, I only had one puff from this cigar. Yet it was the cigar I will never forget.

Left: Cigarette advertisements often used to portray smoking as romantic or sexy.

One fine fall morning in San Francisco. I had taken a cable car from Union Square to the foot of Columbus Street, intending to walk back through the old Italian quarter of North Beach. In a great mood. A week of hard work had gone well, and now I had a couple of days off to myself. So I had gone into Dunhill's and bought the finest cigar in the shop to smoke on an equally fine walk.

If you happen to appreciate cigars, this was a Macanudo, maduro, as big around as my thumb and six-and-a-half inches long—a very serious cigar. If you do not appreciate cigars, this one is best described as one of those cigars that would make you say, "My God, you're not going to smoke that thing in here, are you?"

After a few blocks' walk, it was cigar time. With care I removed the cellophane, squeezed the cigar to check for freshness, and held it to my nose to make sure it wasn't sour. Perfect. Leaning against a tree, I cut the end off the cigar with my pocketknife and carefully lit up. One puff, and I said aloud to myself. "Now that, THAT, is *some* cigar!"

It so happened that I had been standing in front of a coffeehouse. A cup of fine espresso would add the final right ingredient to a recipe for a memorable morning. Placing the lit cigar carefully on the wide brick window ledge of the coffeehouse, I went inside to order. While waiting at the counter, I glanced out the window to check on my cigar. Gone. My cigar was gone.

Abandoning my coffee, I rushed to the door. And stopped short. There on the other side of the glass was an old man examining my cigar with the skill of an aficionado. He held the cigar with respect under his nose and smelled it with eyes closed. He smiled. He squeezed the cigar to check for freshness. He smiled. Looking carefully up and down the street, he took a puff. And smiled again. With a heavenward salute with the cigar, he set off down the street. SMOKING MY CIGAR. I followed, not knowing quite what to do. I really wanted that cigar back.

The old man. Salt-and-pepper hair, with grand mustache and eyebrows to match—jaunty black longshoreman's cap, white long-sleeved shirt, black suspenders, and dark brown pants and shoes. Short, plump, wrinkled, walking with a slight limp, the old man ambled on into the morning, unaware of me lurking furtively a few yards behind.

Italian. First-generation immigrant probably. As were the friends he visited to report the good news of the cigar that fate had prepared for him that fine day. I got a tour of the old Italian quarter of North Beach I had not anticipated—the real thing. A pasta shop, a fruit stand, a hardware store, a bakery, and the local priest.

At each stop, in passionate terms, he exalted the cigar, his good fortune, and this lovely day. Each friend was offered a sample puff. The fruit vendor squeezed the cigar and approved its ripeness. The baker puffed twice and pronounced the cigar "*Primo, primo.*" The priest gave the cigar a mock blessing.

In time the old man turned toward the bocce ball courts north of Ghirardelli Square and when he arrived, he repeated for his compatriots his ritual celebration of the cigar and his good luck. The cigar burned down to a short stub. As it came his turn to play, the old man meditated upon the end of the cigar with clear regret. He did not toss it to the ground and grind it underfoot as I might have. No. Solemnly, he walked over to a flower bed, scooped a small hole beneath a rosebush, laid the cigar butt to rest, covered it with dirt, and patted the small grave smooth with his hand. Pausing, he raised his cap in respect, smiled, and returned to play the game.

The old man may have smoked it, but I've not enjoyed a cigar more. If having a lovely memory is the best possession, then that cigar is still mine, is it not? It remains the finest cigar I never had.

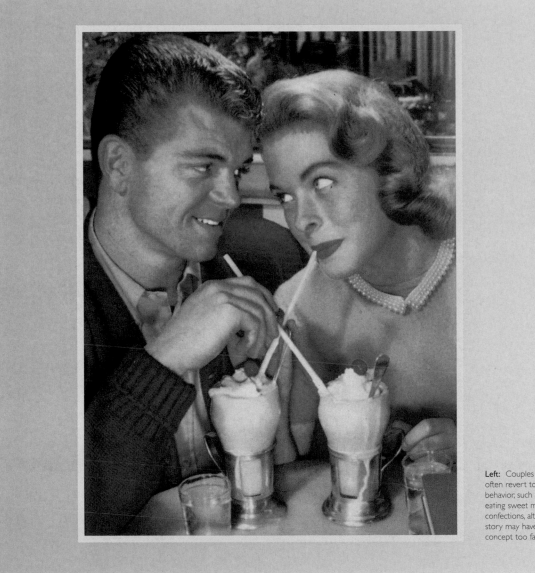

Left: Couples in love often revert to baby-like behavior, such as here eating sweet milky confections, although this story may have taken the concept too far!

DATING   YOUR   MOM

Ian Frazier

IN TODAY'S FAST-MOVING, TRANSIENT, ROOTLESS SOCIETY, WHERE PEOPLE MEET AND make love and part without ever really touching, the relationship every guy already has with his own mother is too valuable to ignore. Here is a grown, experienced, loving woman—one you do not have to go to a party or singles bar to meet, one you do not have to go to great lengths to get to know. There are hundreds of times when you and your mother are thrown together naturally, without the tension that usually accompanies courtship—just the two of you, alone. All you need is a little presence of mind to take advantage of these situations. Say your mom is driving you downtown in the car to buy you a new pair of slacks. First, find a nice station on the car radio, one that she likes. Get into the pleasant lull of freeway driving—tires humming along the pavement, air-conditioner on max. Then turn to look at her across the front seat and say something like, "You know, you've really kept your shape, Mom, and don't think I haven't noticed." Or suppose she comes into your room to bring you some clean socks. Take her by the wrist, pull her close, and say, "Mom, you're the most fascinating woman I've ever met." Probably she'll tell you to cut out the foolishness, but I can guarantee you one thing: she will never tell your dad. Possibly she would find it hard to say, "Dear, Piper just made a pass at me," or possibly she is secretly flattered, but, whatever the reason, she will keep it to herself until the day comes when she is no longer ashamed to tell the world of your love.

Dating your mother seriously might seem difficult at first, but once you try it I'll bet you'll be surprised at how easy it is. Facing up to your intention is the main thing: you have to want it bad enough. One problem is that lots of people get hung up on feelings of guilt about their dad. They think, Oh, here's this kindly old guy who taught me how to hunt and whittle and dynamite fish—I can't let him go on into his twilight years alone. Well, there are two reasons you can dismiss those thoughts from your mind. First, *every* woman, I don't care who she is, prefers her son to her husband. That is a simple fact; ask any woman who has a son, and she'll admit it. And why shouldn't she prefer someone who is so much like herself, who represents nine months of special concern and love and intense physical closeness—someone whom she actually created? As more women begin to express the need to have something all their own in the world, more women are going to start being honest about this preference. When you and your mom begin going together, you will simply become part of a natural and inevitable historical trend.

Second, you must remember this about your dad: you have your mother, he has his! Let him go put the moves on his own mother and stop messing with yours. If his mother is dead or too old to be much use anymore, that's not your fault, is it? It's not your fault that he didn't realize his mom for the woman she was, before it was too late. Probably he's going to try a lot of emotional blackmail on you just because you had a good idea and he never did. Don't buy it. Comfort yourself with the thought that your dad belongs to the last generation of guys who will let their moms slip away from them like that.

Once your dad is out of the picture—once he has taken up fly-tying, joined the Single Again Club, moved to Russia, whatever—and your mom has been wooed and won, if you're anything like me you're going to start having so much fun that the good times you had with your mother when you were little will seem tame by comparison. For a while, Mom and I went along living a contented, quiet life, just happy to be with each other. But after several months we started getting into some different things, like the big motorized stroller. The thrill I felt the first time Mom steered me down the street! On the tray, in addition to my Big Jim doll and the wire with the colored wooden beads, I have my desk blotter, my typewriter, an in-out basket, and my name plate. I get a lot of work done, plus I get a great chance to people-watch. Then there's my big, adult-sized highchair, where I sit in the evening as Mom and I watch the news and discuss current events, while I paddle in my food and throw my dishes on the floor. When Mom reaches to wipe off my chin and I take her hand, and we fall to the floor in a heap—me, Mom, highchair, and all—well, those are the best times, those are the very best times.

It is true that occasionally I find myself longing for even more—for things I know I cannot have, like the feel of a firm, strong, gentle hand at the small of my back lifting me out of bed into the air, or someone who could walk me around and burp me after I've watched all the bowl games and had about nine beers. Ideally, I would like a mom about nineteen or twenty feet tall, and although I considered for a while asking my mom to start working out with weights and drinking Nutrament, I finally figured, Why put her through it? After all, she is not only my woman, she is my best friend. I have to take her as she is, and the way she is plenty good enough for me.

A C K N O W L E D G M E N T S

First and foremost, we would like to thank Jeremy Tarcher for his vision in creating this anthology series, and for his dedication and unwavering support in guiding the book towards completion. Our greatest appreciation is also extended to Robert Bly, Jean Houston, Robert A. Johnson, and Andrew Weil for their essential contributions to this series. To John Beebe, editor of the *San Francisco Institute Library Journal,* Alan B. Chinen, Connie Zweig, and the many members of the Jungian, transpersonal, and holistic medicine communities for their insights and suggestions concerning the selection of materials for these books—our deepest thanks. The talents of several people came together to make this unique collection of stories and art into the beautiful volume you hold in your hands. Mark Robert Waldman, whose skills as an author and editor shine in the choices he made for the book, carefully selected the texts. Julie Foakes, whose talents as an art researcher can never be praised enough, chose all the images. Marion Kocot brought order and harmony to the words with her talented editing skills. Sara Carder at Tarcher Putnam provided constant encouragement and handholding throughout the process. Joel Fontinos, the publisher at Tarcher Putnam, guided us with enthusiasm and praise. And Kristen Garneau brought text and images together in the elegant layout of the pages. To you all A HUGE THANK YOU!

—Philip and Manuela Dunn of The Book Laboratory Inc.

ABOUT THE EDITOR

Mark Robert Waldman is a therapist and the author and editor of numerous books, including *The Spirit of Writing, Love Games, Dreamscaping* and *The Art of Staying Together.* He was founding editor of *Transpersonal Review,* covering the fields of transpersonal and Jungian psychology, religious studies, and mind/body medicine.

ABOUT THE BOOK CREATORS

Philip Dunn and Manuela Dunn Mascetti have created many best-selling volumes, including *The Illustrated Rumi,* Huston Smith's *Illustrated World's Religions,* Stephen Hawking's *The Illustrated A Brief History of Time* and *The Universe in a Nutshell,* and Thomas Moore's *The Illustrated Care of the Soul.* They are the authors of *The Illustrated Rumi, The Buddha Box,* and many other books.

ABOUT THE INTRODUCTORY AUTHOR

Robert A. Johnson is a noted lecturer and Jungian analyst. He is the author of *Ecstasy: Understanding the Psychology of Joy, Inner Work,* and three related volumes—*He, She,* and *We*—which explore the psychology of men, women, and romantic love.

T E X T   A C K N O W L E D G M E N T S

Every effort has been made to trace all copyright holders of the material included in this volume, whether companies or individuals. Any omission is unintentional and we will be pleased to correct any errors in future editions of this book.

The Cigar, from *Uh-Oh* by Robert Fulghum, © 1991 by Robert Fulghum. Reproduced by kind permission of Villard Books, a division of Random House, Inc.

The Date, originally published in *The Sun*, © 1999 and 2001 by Brenda Miller. Used by kind permission of the author

Dating Your Mom, © 1997 by *The New Yorker*. Used by kind permission of The Wylie Agency, Inc.

The Boy by Joyce Carol Oates, © 1988 by Ontario Review Press Inc. Used by kind permission of John Hawkins & Associates, Inc.

a fourth of july, © 2001 by Joe Balay. Used by kind permission of the author

Frankie and Johnnie, traditional folk ballad, retold by Mark Robert Waldman, ©2001 by Mark Robert Waldman. Used by kind permission of the author

Girls in Their Summer Dresses. Reprinted with permission, © 1978 by Irwin Shaw. All Rights Reserved

Innocence in Extremis, © 1998 by Debra Boxer. Used by kind permission of the author

The Kiss, originally appeared in *75 Story Masterpieces*, Bantam Books, 1961, © 1961 by William Sansom, renewed 1989 by Nicholas C. Sansom. Used by kind permission of Russell & Volkening as agents for the author

A R T   A C K N O W L E D G M E N T S

Page 11   Andrew Lane

Page 17   Getty Images/Hulton Archive

Page 22   Ivan Albright, American, 1897-1983, *Hail to the Pure,* 1977, lithograph, 44.3 x 32.4 cm,
                 Earle Ludgin Bequest, 1981.1161, photo reproduction © The Art Institute of Chicago. All
                 Rights Reserved

Page 23   Julie Foakes

Page 27   Sarah Pletts, *Angus cuddling me,* 1986, ink and charcoal on paper

Page 28   Ivan Albright, American, 1897-1983, *Nude,* 1931, oil on canvas, 35.6 x 18.1 cm, Mary and
                 Earle Ludgin Collection, 1981.256, photo reproduction © The Art Institute of Chicago. All
                 Rights Reserved

Page 30   Andrew Lane

Page 31   Richard Maris Loving, American, b. 1929, *Untitled,* 1959, enamel and copper on wood, Gift
                 of Frederick S. Livingston Jr. Frank Livingstone and Sally L., 1991.597, photo reproduction ©
                 The Art Institute of Chicago. All Rights Reserved

Page 34   Barry Peterson, *H-F Gesture #10,* 18" x 24", compressed charcoal on bond

Page 37   Mary Evans Picture Library

Page 40   Getty Images/Hulton Archive

Page 42   Mary Evans Picture Library

Page 49   Courtesy of The Advertising Archives

Page 50   Getty Images/Hulton Archive

Page 51   Mary Evans Picture Library

Page 55   Getty Images/Hulton Archive

Page 56   Courtesy of The Advertising Archives

Page 61   Andrew Lane, *Beauty is in the Eye of the Beholder*

Page 62   Louis Barlow, *Jitterbugs*, 1939, wood engraving; 1989.11, Amon Carter Museum, Fort Worth, Texas

Page 65   Andrew Lane

Page 70   Getty Images/Hulton Archive

Page 71   Mary Evans Picture Library

Page 72   Agnes Pelton, *Untitled,* 1931, oil on canvas, 36 1/8 x 24 1/8 in. (91.76 x 61.28 cm.), framed 37 5/16 x 25 7/16 in. Whitney Museum of American Art, New York; purchase, with funds from the Modern Painting and Sculpture Committee 96.175

Page 76   Courtesy of The Advertising Archives

Page 77   Alfred Stieglitz, American 1864-1946, *Dorothy True*, 1919, chloride print, 24 x 19.2 cm, The Alfred Stieglitz Collection, 1949.720. Reproduction © The Art Institute of Chicago. All Rights Reserved

Page 80   Julie Foakes

Page 85   Mary Evans Picture Library

Page 121   Philip Guston, American, 1913-1980, *Couple in Bed,* 1977, oil on canvas, 205.7 x 240 cm, Through prior bequest of Frances W. Pick, restricted gift of Mrs. Harold Hines, 1989.435, photo reproduction © The Art Institute of Chicago. All Rights Reserved. Courtesy the artist's estate.

Page 124   Georgia O'Keeffe, American, 1887-1986. White Shell with Red, 1938, pastel on wood pulp laminate board, 54.6 x 69.8 cm, Alfred Stieglitz Collection, bequest of Georgia O'Keeffe, 1987.250.5, photo reproduction © The Art Institute of Chicago. All Rights Reserved

Page 127   Sarah Pletts, *Stephen at the basin,* 1984, acrylic on board, 24" x 48"

Page 128   Vin Mag Archive

Page 132   Courtesy of The Advertising Archives